THIS IS
THE RITUAL

To Antoinette and Jimmy Doyle

THIS IS
THE RITUAL
ROB DOYLE

THE LILLIPUT PRESS
DUBLIN

This is the Ritual, The Dublin Edition
published by
THE LILLIPUT PRESS
62–63 Sitric Road, Arbour Hill,
Dublin 7, Ireland
www.lilliputpress.ie

Copyright © Rob Doyle, 2016

A CIP record for this title is available
from The British Library.

1 3 5 7 9 10 8 6 4 2

ISBN 978 1 84351 669 9

Set in 10 pt on 15 pt Trump Mediaeval by Marsha Swan
Printed in Spain by GraphyCems

Contents

John-Paul Finnegan, Paltry Realist

When I think of Ireland, John-Paul Finnegan said as we stood on the deck of the ferry while it pulled out of Holyhead, I think of a limitless ignorance. And not just an ignorance, but a *wallowing* in ignorance, akin to the wallowing in filth of a pig or a naked, demented savage. Ireland and the people of Ireland wallow in ignorance much in the way that a child or a lunatic wallows in its own filth, smearing the walls with it, grinning and cooing loudly, smearing the walls and itself with its own filth, its own stinking self-made filth. This is definitely how the Irish people are, he said. This is their primary characteristic. Absolutely. Elsewhere in the world you can find qualities in people, both individuals and groups, which correspond to words such as spirit, life-force, vitality, passion and curiosity, but in Ireland you will find no such qualities. No such qualities at all. This is what John-Paul Finnegan, author of *Nevah Trust a Christian*, told me as the ferry, the *Ulysses*, began to

1

move out of the harbour at Holyhead, propelling itself away from the British coast, towards Dublin.

Consider the name of this very ship, said John-Paul Finnegan. In fact, don't even get me started on the name of this ship, he said. But it was too late, because he had already got himself started on the name of the ship, which was *Ulysses*. Not a single fucking dickhead in all of Ireland has actually read *Ulysses*, said John-Paul Finnegan. Except me, of course, the biggest dickhead of them all. Yet everyone in Ireland pretends to have read *Ulysses*, or acts like they've read it, but none of them have. The last person in Ireland to read *Ulysses* was James Joyce, and even he only read half of it, said John-Paul Finnegan. Come to think of it, there were a few professors who came after Joyce who also read *Ulysses*, or rather, they didn't read it, they *killed* it, they killed *Ulysses* by James Joyce, just like they have killed almost every other book that was once worth reading. And not only did they kill *Ulysses*, but first they mutilated it, subjecting it to the most mental forms of torture. And how did they kill it? he asked. I will tell you, he said. They killed *Ulysses* by rendering it a desiccated literary relic; they wrote a slew of murderously dull articles about *Ulysses*, and thereby killed it. They killed *Ulysses* by making it seem to anyone unfortunate or depraved enough to read one of their hateful papers that *Ulysses* is the most boring and flaccid book in the world, when of course it is anything but the most boring and flaccid book in the world, it is in fact deeply subversive, scatological, irreverent, perverse, and above all, diabolically deviant. That is, the form and the content of the book are deviant: they deviate from good taste, from literary classicism, from the boredoms of morality and plot, and from sentimentality – in other words, from *all the shit of literature*, said John-Paul Finnegan, the typical and all-too-prevalent *shit*

2

of literature. Like any decent author, said John-Paul Finnegan, Joyce ignored the shit, he sidestepped it, *the hideous shit of literature*, because he couldn't be bothered and he wanted to write a new kind of book, which is the only thing worth doing if you call yourself a writer of any description. Yet if you read one of the papers, *any* of the papers by those *unconscionable fucking dickheads* who write about *Ulysses*, you will soon if not immediately come to the conclusion that this book, this *Ulysses*, is not worth reading precisely because, judging by how these *academic fucks*, these *sick, life-hating, evil, mental, and spiritually crippled fucks* write about it, *Ulysses* must be the least interesting of all books, said John-Paul Finnegan as the ship, the *Ulysses*, finally pulled out of the harbour and commenced upon open water.

I sighed. John-Paul Finnegan was right, I thought. But then again, maybe he wasn't right. Maybe he was entirely wrong, as he had so often been entirely wrong before, about so many things, nearly everything in fact. After all, *I* had read *Ulysses*, so he wasn't entirely right. Likelier he was entirely wrong. After all, I was Irish, and I had read *Ulysses*. What about me? I said to John-Paul Finnegan, suddenly indignant that he would so casually disparage the entirety of the Irish race, myself included, on the basis of such a truly sweeping generalisation. What about me? I said again. To which John-Paul Finnegan looked at me, clasping his hands as the ship cut across the waves. What about you? he said warily. I read *Ulysses*, I said. That's right, he said, I'd forgotten that. He seemed to be having a moment of self-doubt. So there's you and then there's me and then there's James Joyce, he said finally. We three have all read *Ulysses*. But no one else in Ireland has ever read *Ulysses*, he added. This I know. I know this simply because I know it, he said, his confidence returning. In other words it is what the philosophers call *a priori* knowledge, the kind of knowledge which we can possess prior to, indeed independently of, empirical verification. I simply *know*, as you know, as everybody knows, that everyone in Ireland, everyone except you and me, is too fucking dim-witted, too altogether stupid and moronic, and above all too terrified by the very word *literature*, to have bothered to read *Ulysses*. That's how I know. You think I'm fucking joking, he said, jabbing a finger in my chest. I am not fucking joking, he said. I am not even exaggerating, let alone joking. Irishmen are terrified of the word *literature*. I can guarantee you that if I were to suddenly turn around, on this deck, with these couples and old drunken builders and traveller families and whatnot, and if I were then to roar the word *literature* at the top of my lungs, the vast majority of these people would run to the sides of the ship and hurl themselves over the edge to be drowned. They would sooner drown than confront a man roaring *literature*. And the rest of them, John-Paul Finnegan added, would simply collapse on the spot, they would die of the sheer horror that the word *literature* provoked in them, the boundless sense of nausea, terror and repulsion it provoked in their Irish hearts, that is to say their *pig-hearts*, their *flaccid dickhead hearts*. Some of them would have heart attacks, others aneurysms. Others would simply keel, causes unknown. For they know nothing of literature, of Joyce, and they care for less, these Irishmen, said John-Paul Finnegan, glowering at me now with a ferocity and yes, a hatred which I had done nothing to deserve, or so I felt. I may as well roar *Allahu akbar*, added John-Paul Finnegan, as roar *literature*. I may as well wrap a towel around my head and roar *Allahu akbar* while ripping off my shirt to reveal a suicide vest, as to roar *literature*, for the effect it would have on these Irishmen, in other words these cretins, these fuckheads, these unconscionable morons and idiots, these fucking heartless and mindless pricks, these pigs and sheep and rodents that call themselves Irishmen, when in truth they should call themselves sheep and pigs and rodents, if not total fucking spanners, said John-Paul Finnegan, who now had flecks of foam collecting at the corners of his mouth, and whose eyes had not left mine. But it seemed to me that the boundless hate had drained from John-Paul Finnegan's eyes, and what remained was a childlike fear, a pleading, a remorse even. I imagined that John-Paul Finnegan was flailing out in the sea, not the Irish Sea which our ship, the *Ulysses*, was cutting across at a decent speed, but the metaphorical sea, the Black Sea or the Dead Sea, the sea of loneliness, self-hate and dread that is the fate not of all men, but certainly of all *thinking* men, as John-Paul Finnegan had himself told me, in one of his more vulnerable moments, when we had lived together in London, in a crowded and unsanitary house near Finsbury Park.

These pricks! he shouted. These unconscionable mental pricks! How I fucking loathe them, he muttered, shaking his head violently, too violently I thought, he might do himself damage. He drew sharply from his hip-flask, neglecting to pass it to me. How low can you go? he asked. How fucking low? I will tell you how low: all the way to Ireland. That's how low you can fucking go. I let it pass, that inane comment, and fell to thinking about our lives in London, the lives we were leaving behind, standing as we were on the deck of this ship, this *Ulysses* that was cutting across the Irish Sea, the coast of Britain fading behind us. It was in the house near Finsbury Park that John-Paul Finnegan had written the last three volumes of *Nevah Trust a Christian*, his *novel in eleven volumes*, as he always called it, with bottomless perversity, the fact being that there were no fewer than *thirteen* volumes in his novel, if it even was a novel. I had moved into the house when John-Paul Finnegan was nearing the end of volume twelve, which he had titled *Who's Ya Daddy?* I write eight thousand words per day, he had told me on the night we first went out for drinks in the Twelve Pins pub on Seven Sisters Road. I replied that eight thousand words seemed like a lot, in fact it seemed like far too many words to write in a single day. Absolutely fucking correct, it is too many, it's far too many words even for the most deadline-haunted hack, let alone for a writer of literature, such as myself, John-Paul Finnegan said, pouring a shot of whiskey into his Guinness, as was his wont, a concoction which he called *Guinnskey*. It was then that John-Paul Finnegan had explained to me his notion of *paltry realism*, the genre in which he claimed to write, and which he also claimed to have invented. Paltry realism means writing shit, he said. What I mean to say is, what is art, only a howl against death. Are we agreed on this, Rob? he demanded. I nodded my head. Good, he said. Then we are agreed that art is a howl against death and nothing more. Yet why is it, he said, that so much art tries to do the opposite, to ignore, even to deny death? Have you thought about this? he asked. Art, and especially literature, has a thousand clever ways of denying or ignoring death. One of these ways is literariness itself, that is, literary imposture, said John-Paul Finnegan. By which I mean the ceaseless attempt by practitioners of literature to achieve beauty and perfection, to write well, in short *to craft perfect and elegant sentences*. This is infinite bollocks, said John-Paul Finnegan. If you write slowly, carefully, then what are you doing if not indulging in vanity – the *vanity of writing well*. It's no different from wearing a nice coat or a frock or a shiny pair of shoes to a *bourgeois* dinner party – and I will tell you now, he added, I am not nor have I ever been the kind of man to attend dinner parties, *bourgeois* or otherwise. And death is no fucking dinner party. The point is, though, said John-Paul Finnegan, trying to write well is vanity and nothing other than vanity, and when I say vanity I essentially mean *the fear of death expressed in self-framing*, as you will have guessed. That is where the technique of paltry realism makes its stance. Paltry realism means writing rapidly, and yes, even writing badly, in fact only writing badly, and not seeking to impress anyone with your writing, with either its style or its content. Paltry realism means writing eight thousand words per day, he said. Eight thousand words – far too many for any *decent or tasteful writer*, but perfect for the practitioner of paltry realism, a school which, for the time being, consists solely of me, said John-Paul Finnegan, fixing another Guinnskey. I was intrigued by his theory of paltry realism and urged him to say more, though I needn't have bothered, as he was already talking over me, caught up in the swell of his own oratory, aflame with the zeal I was to observe in him many times over the course of our friendship, which began that night in the Twelve Pins and continued to the afternoon when we stood together on the deck of the *Ulysses*, which was now at full steam as it tore across the Irish Sea, the British coastline having faded completely to the stern. Another indicator of the vanity and ultimately the self-delusion of literature, even in its so-called avant-garde, modernist or experimental guises, is that its practitioners invariably display a craving, a very unseemly craving, to have their work published, John-Paul Finnegan had said that night in the pub, him downing Guinnskeys and me downing Guinnesses. All of them, the brazen slags, all they want is to be published, he said. They want an adoring or a scandalised public to read their works, thereby granting them a kind of immortality, or so they would like to think. This goes for Céline, Kafka, Pessoa, Joyce, Marinetti, Musil, Markson, Handke, Hamsun, Stein, Sebald, Bernhard, Ballard, Beckett, Blanchot, Burroughs, Bolaño, Cioran, Duras, Gombrowicz, Pound, Eliot, and any other dickhead of the so-called avant-garde that you might care to mention, as much as it goes for McEwan, Self, Banville, Tóibín, Auster, Atwood, Ellis, Amis, Thirlwell, Hollinghurst, Smith, Doyle, Dyer, Franzen, and any other arsehole active in mainstream literature today, said John-Paul Finnegan. To them, the value of a work of literature is dependent on its being published. If it is not published, it has no value. There is an ontological question at work here, he added: if a book is unread by anyone except its author, can it be said to exist? More pertinently, can it be said to be any good? My response, and paltry realism's response, is simply to bypass the whole squalid agenda. What is the point in sending my writing out to publishers, said John-Paul Finnegan, so that they might accept or reject it? What is the use in that? I will tell you now: *I* reject the publishers, every last one of them, even the ones I admire, the ones I revere, the good and the best of them, because I am a paltry realist, and publication, Rob, is not among my aims, not among my aims at all, it is not among my aims, I am simply not fucking interested in being published, he said, slamming his Guinnskey on the table. I write for other reasons, he added, though he neglected to say what they were. On several occasions, while we were living together in the house near Finsbury Park, John-Paul Finnegan had permitted me to read sections of *Nevah Trust a Christian*, his gargantuan work allegedly in the paltry realist mode. True enough, the writing was very bad, and obviously written in great haste (handwritten, that is – John-Paul Finnegan hated typing on a laptop). The prose was utterly devoid of literary flair and displayed not the slightest effort to seduce or entertain the reader. Not that the writing was *hostile* to the reader, as can be the case among the severest of modernists; rather, the writing seemed *indifferent* to the reader, perhaps even unaware of the reader's existence. There were few paragraph breaks and no chapter breaks. There was no discernible story and no characters. The word *fuck*, or one of its variants, appeared at least once on every line, more often twice or three times, or more. The word *cunt* was almost as frequent; the words *bastard*, *dickhead*, *rodent* and *moron* riddled the text. Several pages consisted solely of *fuck*-derived words repeated hundreds of times, punctuated by *bastard, mongrel, cunthawk* or *dickhead*. Others offered perfunctory descriptions of dusty towns and hurtling trams, giant mounds of waste and crumbling ridges, or glibly vicious references to contemporary events. I had the sense of an inner monologue; not exactly a stream of consciousness, more like a machine gun of consciousness, or a self-bludgeoning of consciousness, or just an interminable, pointless spewing of language, a kind of insane vomiting of language, page after page of it, a dozen volumes stacked on the floor beside John-Paul Finnegan's desk, which was a backstage dressing table salvaged from a closed-down strip club.

But this is not even the worst of it, John-Paul Finnegan said suddenly as we stood together on the deck of the *Ulysses* as it bounced over the waves, away from Britain. This ship, this *Ulysses*, is not even the worst of it, he repeated. The worst of it is *Bloomsday*. Have you ever seen Bloomsday? he asked. What I'm talking about, he said, is the national day of celebration in tribute to a book that no one in Ireland has *even fucking read*! That is what I refer to, said John-Paul Finnegan. Until a decade or so ago, Bloomsday was merely a kind of minor national stain, a silly and moronic venture that no one really bothered with, and which you could safely ignore. But then the government, that gang of dribbling pricks, that *moron collective*, as I have so often labelled them, saw in Bloomsday a serious marketing opportunity, one which they, in their infinite hatefulness, decided was far too lucrative to ignore. There was more money to be squeezed out of Joyce, they decided, as if Joyce were a sponge or a testicle, and even though not one of them – this I know – not one of them had ever read *Ulysses*, or even *Dubliners*, or any of Joyce's books at all, said John-Paul Finnegan. In fact, these morons that I'm referring to, these are the kind of people who, if you suggested to them that they might read *Ulysses* or *Dubliners*, would laugh out loud. And I'm not talking about an embarrassed or a *social* form of laughter, he said, but a *bellowing, hearty and spontaneous* laughter, from the guts, a laughter of delight at what they would consider the mad and uproarious idea of reading *Ulysses* or *Dubliners*, said John-Paul Finnegan. He drew again from his hip-flask, then passed it to me. I drank. These morons, these dickheads, these unconscionable fucking arseholes decided to commercialise this so-called Bloomsday, said John-Paul Finnegan, the day when the fictional Leopold Bloom fictionally wandered around Dublin city, drinking, ruminating, chatting and so on. In other words, the sixteenth of June, he said. It would bring in the tourists, they reckoned. It would bring in the Yanks and Japs, the French and the Germans, the Swedes and the Slavs, the vulgarian Bulgarians and the roaming Romanians, and all those grinning tourists would spend their money admiring *the Irish people* and their literary heritage, even though the people of Ireland no longer read, are too stupid to read, let alone to read *Ulysses*, the book that this whole moronic fiasco of Bloomsday purports to cele-brate. You don't need me, said John-Paul Finnegan, to point out that the two Irish writers widely considered the greatest of the twentieth century, even by people who have never read and never intend to read either of them, namely Beckett and Joyce, had nothing but hatred and disgust for Ireland, and for the Irish. These two writers spent a huge amount of energy *actively disparaging* the Irish and Ireland, said John-Paul Finnegan, in their letters and conversation, and frequently in their published work too. Yet here we have a situation, this so-called Bloomsday, wherein all the fat waddling morons on the island gather in the streets to celebrate a book by Joyce which they never bothered to read! Pink pudgy dickheads. Mindless flabby wankers, trailing their moron progeny. Useless bastards one and all. They celebrate *Ulysses* in the most nauseatingly self-conscious of ways, prancing about for the snapping tourists, dancing like twats, like true dickheads for these snapping tourists, who gaze on in a euphoria of mindlessness, clicking their cameras, their smartphone cameras, their video cameras, recording the Irish, *this literary nation*, making absolute fools of themselves by aping the characters in a book they have never read, a book they never intend to read, for they hate books, they hate all books regardless of provenance, the only exceptions being *Harry Potter* and football biographies, said John-Paul Finnegan. Bloomsday, he said, shaking his head in disgust. Bloomsday. Fucking Bloomsday. Blooms-fucking-day. Bloom-fuckings-day. Fuck off, he said. Fuck right off. I mean it, fuck all the world. Listen to this, John-Paul Finnegan said. A few years ago I was back in Dublin, don't ask me why, I was back in Dublin at the time of *Bloomsday*. I went into town, not to partake in the celebrations of course, but for unrelated reasons. And while I was in there I walked up O'Connell Street and listen to this, it will sound like the stuff of broad satire or lunatic fantasy but it is neither, Rob, I assure you. I walked on to O'Connell Street and what did I see, along the pedestrian island running up the middle of Dublin's great thoroughfare, but hundreds of fat grinning idiots, together with their chortling wives and their chubby, shrieking children, all sitting in rows along either side of an immensely long dining table, said John-Paul Finnegan. I am not kidding you. And listen to this. Over their heads was a massive dangling banner, a dangling banner that read *Denny Sausages Celebrate James Joyce's Bloomsday*. Yes! *Denny* fucking *Sausages*! As if the sausages themselves were bursting in ecstasy. This because somewhere in the scat-ological sprawl of *Ulysses*, between its intimate depictions of flatulence, defecation, masturbation, blasphemy, and unbri-dled male and female lust, there is brief mention made of *Denny* fucking *Sausages*, said John-Paul Finnegan. So here they were, hundreds of these fat chortling twats, crowded around a long dining table replete with white tablecloth, being served plate upon plate of sausages, each of them *cram-ming their faces* with sausage, a veritable orgy of sausage-gorging in honour of James Joyce, high-modernist and high-mocker of Ireland. *Here is your legacy, James Joyce*, John-Paul Finnegan roared over the waves, *here is your legacy – two hundred chortling fucks eating sausages! You have really left your fucking mark, James Joyce. Oh yes you have! You are the KING OF MODERNISM!* Presently John-Paul Finnegan produced his hipflask, swigged on it, and passed it to me. I drank self-consciously, for despite the roar of the turbines and the waves crashing against the prow, many of the other travellers on deck had heard John-Paul Finnegan's outburst and were looking warily in our direction. John-Paul Finnegan was oblivious to their gazes, or just indifferent. Fat waddling pricks, he muttered, more subdued now. How they waddle.

Like fat, mental penguins. Fat chortling penguins, grinning like lunatics. Penguins of depravity, penguins of hate. Will I tell you what I did? he said, turning to me sharply. I will tell you what I did. I made it my business to at least attempt to fathom this unprecedented display of public idiocy, this linking of high-modernism to pork consumption. I walked along the rows of chortling, sausage-cramming Dubliners, through the gauntlet of snapping Japs, the lens-faced legions. Then I stopped and asked one woman who was sitting with a pile of sausages on a plate in front of her, whether she had actually read *Ulysses*, said John-Paul Finnegan. She stared at me for a long time, her expression conveying the sheerest bewilderment and horror. Her child began to cry. Eventually the woman came out of her trance, and she said to me, very slowly, *Ulysses*. Just the word *Ulysses*, nothing more. I never saw a woman so afraid. Her little boy had his head in his hands now, weeping through his fingers, wailing. That was when the father turned around. He looked me in the eye, a long and disdainful look it was. Then he said, *I think you'd better leave*. What the fuck, said John-Paul Finnegan, recollecting the incident. What the fuck? All I had done was ask her if she had read *Ulysses*. They ran me out of there, he said. They'd have lynched me, that sausage-mob, if I had not made off with myself. A black day for Ireland, and a black day for me, said John-Paul Finnegan. And yet here I am, here we are, on a ferry, on the fucking *Ulysses* no less, gliding across the sea not away from, but *in the direction of* the accursed land, the steaming hole, the potato field, the literary and intellectual *silence* of Ireland. Would that it would crumble into the sea, he added. Would that the entire stinking mass, the whole abominable island would groan, keel and tumble into the sea. Dissolve in the sea. Dissolve like a man who is made of salt, a man who fell into the sea, he said. He was silent for a time, looking out at the waves. I thought about London, about Dublin, about our position now, suspended between the two cities. We must be the only two Irishmen returning to Ireland rather than fleeing from it, I reflected, not for the first time. I thought about Irish pubs, the many of them back in London I had drunk in with John-Paul Finnegan, and it seemed to me now that they weren't pubs at all, but cages, or bear traps. I began to fantasise about climbing the rail and flinging myself to the sea, vanishing in the foam with a truncated yell.

The journey was nearing its end. John-Paul Finnegan was muttering away by my side, as if in tense dialogue with the waves, or the treacherous forms that squirmed inside his head. I sensed that the closer we got to Dublin, the less sure of himself he became. Very soon we would be at Dublin port. I could already make out the Poolbeg towers hazed on the horizon. I thought of all the time we had spent away, John-Paul Finnegan and I, and the hatred he bore within him, the hatred that is purer than any other, the hatred for where one comes from. And now John-Paul Finnegan turned to me, gripping the rail. I could feel his gaze on me. I turned to face him. What the fuck did they do to me? he said quietly, referring to what, I did not know. What the fuck did they do to me, Rob? The words had to them a tone of revelation. The coastline was expanding across the horizon, sinister and domineering. John-Paul Finnegan shook his head. What the fuck did they do to me? What the fuck was going on, Rob? What the fuck was going on?

I turned away, facing the coast. Neither of us spoke for a time. John-Paul Finnegan went to speak again but hesitated. I did not look at him. Finally he said, I hate what I've written.

I hate every word of it. That moronic and sickening fucking book. That so-called novel which I hate more than anything. He seemed calmer now, even as the coast grew closer, firmer, filling our vision to the prow of the *Ulysses*. Paltry realism is nothing, means nothing, he said. I wrote what I wrote because I thought it would heal me, but there is no healing, you just learn to live with your wounds and your mutilations, and you stagger onwards, crippled and bedraggled, towards your death. One day your energy fails you and you keel over, and that's that. You have not been healed. In a way you died from your wounds. Every hurt and every humiliation lasts for ever. There is no healing. Writing changes nothing, it's an infliction. You inflict yourself on the page, and then on the reader, and on the world. Better to have no readers, better not to write at all. There was no worth to what I wrote, nor to anything I have ever done. Nothing in my life has had any worth. Writing has no worth. Nothing has any worth. Nothing. We were both silent as the ferry sailed into the mouth of the port, the twin red and white towers looming like sentries. Now John-Paul Finnegan seemed truly calm, self-possessed once more, neither raging nor afraid. I will not forgive, he said. Fuck it all. I have decided. I will not forgive them, not forgive any of them for what they have done, for what they have done to me. I will not forgive them, he said. I will not. No. Fuck it, he said.

No Man's Land

At a certain point in my early twenties, a severe nervous affliction that I had been struggling against for many long months finally overwhelmed me. I was forced to drop out of university, quit my part-time job as a security guard at a stalled building development on the outskirts of the city, and move back in with my parents.

For two months I rarely left the house. I spent my days in bed, or shuffling between the rooms, hallway and landing in a medicated daze. My mother took temporary leave of her job as a secretary so she could stay at home to make me cups of tea and meals of soup, fruit and pasta, which I no more than poked at. On several occasions I walked in on her weeping in the kitchen, or in the cemented back garden that was hidden from the neighbours by high, grey-brick walls. Sometimes I heard her weeping in the bathroom. She always tried to hide her crying from me.

Reading, during this period, was impossible; the letters on the page were alive and crackling, mocking my inability to organise their scattered chaos into some semblance of meaning. I tried instead to watch television, or films on DVD, but everything that came through the screen was unbearably sinister – a spewing of cruelty, bewilderment and chaos that, I realized, other people consumed with utter nonchalance, day after day.

I passed the better part of my days playing games on the Xbox, an activity which somehow left me free of the anxieties aroused by books or television. After two and a half months, I began to feel up to taking walks. For the first few days my walks lasted only twenty or thirty minutes, taking me no further than the few blocks of dreary, featureless working-class suburb around my parents' house and the shadowy park nearby. Walking in this area where I had grown up and to which I had always felt deeply alien, largely but not solely on account of the miseries of victimisation I'd had to endure there for years as an awkward, painfully sensitive and somewhat effeminate boy, served mainly to awaken buried traumas which exacerbated the agony I was already in.

Deciding I needed to go further afield, I began to conduct my walks on the Ballymount estate, which I had heard described as the largest industrial estate in western Europe. The estate begins at the limits of Bluebell and Clondalkin, two depressed suburbs on the south-western peripheries of Dublin. It stretches out for miles, strewn with warehouses, disused factories, and other low, anonymous buildings whose purpose was and remains unknown to me. Between the clusters of buildings, which are spaced far enough apart for realms of unearthly silence to predominate in the landscape, there are high metal railings and fences, stretches of rubble and scrub, and shapeless swathes of long and withered grass.

When I was seventeen, I had worked part-time on the industrial estate, at a table in a windowless room in a long, rectangular building, separating money-off supermarket coupons into discrete piles. Before my evening shifts, I would always stand outside, at a secluded corner of the building, and gaze through a fog of hash-smoke at the void of the Ballymount landscape. It must have been these stoned observances that imbued the place with such haunting resonance for me during my two miserable years in university, when I longed for it with an intense nostalgia.

I started to take the bus out to Ballymount almost every day, in the late morning or early afternoon. My mother was tentatively hopeful that the increased vitality evidenced by my leaving the house was a sign of recovery. I never told her where I was going; I thought it more prudent to say I was heading into the city centre, where (I suggested) it would do me good to merge with the crowds, or sit in cafés, or browse in bookshops. On some days I took my Discman out to the estate, listening as I wandered to formless ambient soundscapes that deepened my sense of being in a place that was beyond the world, and which now outlived it, a timeless zone of litter and intermittent wind. Other days I would borrow pop CDs dating from my younger sister's teenage years. It gave me a peculiar feeling to stand alone in the windswept emptiness of Ballymount and experience, with Michael Jackson or Destiny's Child pulsing in my ears, the gulf between the exuberant commotion of civilization and the vast ruination that had swept over it – for there in Ballymount industrial estate, it took little imagination to believe that the catastrophe had already happened.

I spent three, four, five hours there each day, and for weeks I avoided all human contact; I kept to the blank stretches

18

between zones of activity, the overgrown margins that were silent but for the odd car streaking across the unseen distance. Whenever I saw far-off figures mutely conducting business outside warehouses or unloading trucks, I turned away, straying deeper into the emptiness of the estate.

One dull midweek afternoon, walking while lost as ever in convoluted and intractable worry, I looked up and saw an unexpected form in the distance. It was a man, standing alone on the dull-brown, stony wasteland far ahead of me, out beyond a cluster of run-down buildings. I had been walking randomly, as usual, following no trail but that dictated by my whims. Now I stopped and peered across the empty stretch. The man was facing away from me, gazing at the horizon. As I walked a little closer, I saw that his hair was wildly unkempt, thinning and scraggly, blown by the wind in wayward streaks across his protuberant forehead and bone-angled face. It is difficult to say whether the following is a genuine memory, or if my subsequent encounters with the man retroactively tainted my recollections, but when I think of it now, I feel strongly that my first sight of him provoked in me a deep chill – a sense of total abjection and an urge to flee. Whatever I really did feel, I diverted my walk, that first day, to keep me well away from the solitary figure on the Ballymount estate.

Two days later, he was there again. I was wandering in a different area of the estate, deeper into it, where it becomes harder to tell where you are. The man was walking on his own. He had his hands in his pockets and I could see that he was muttering to himself. When I was about twenty metres away he looked up and saw me. After I had passed him by I heard a call, muffled by a wind that had just then started up. I turned back and he was watching me. His gaze seemed hungry, desperate, as if he craved to take something from me.

The man gestured for me to approach him and I did. He was a lot older than me, perhaps in his late thirties. His clothes were faded, as if they'd been worn for so long that all the colours had bled into the same indefinite non-colour as the man who wore them. He took out a pouch of tobacco and started to roll a smoke. 'Do ye want one?' he said. His voice seemed hollow, as if there was no one behind it. I wanted to walk away, but I nodded and muttered, 'Yeah, please,' even though I'd stopped smoking. He gave me the cigarette, then rolled another for himself. It took him only a couple of seconds to roll them. His fingertips were stained a thick yellow and his nails were caked with dirt. He lit my smoke, then his own. He sat down on his hunkers, facing across the wasteland towards the murk where the sun was sinking, heavy and lifeless, jaded with the world.

'What's your name?' said the man. The question sounded unnatural, as though the speaker were trying to replicate the conversational patterns of a species among whom he was exiled, and whose experience was inscrutable to him.

I told him my name. He asked me why I was walking around Ballymount. I shrugged and mumbled that I just took walks, I needed to clear my head.

'I know what ye mean,' he said. 'It's the same way for me.'

He opened the tattered schoolbag he had on his back and took out a can of Dutch Gold. He handed it to me and opened another for himself. I stood there with the can, sipping from it, looking at the ground. 'I come out here and listen to the place,' he said. 'The humming of it. And the spirits from the old Ireland underneath. Ye can still hear them, just about.' He looked sideways at me, gauging my reaction. Though I had just met him, I felt that I could either crush or elate him by whatever I did next.

I nodded my head.

He smoked hard on his roll-up, turning away from me towards a cluster of deserted-looking buildings. He finished his can and opened a new one (I was still on my first couple of sips).

'What do ye know about Nietzsche?' he said.

I didn't know what to answer. I mumbled that I knew a bit, not much, God is dead.

'Nietzsche didn't see this coming,' he said, ignoring my response. 'Or he did, but he didn't know how bad it would get. He thought this was a transition, he still held out the hope for some kind of breakthrough. The laughter that would ring out across the planet. As if we could find a home again. But we can't. There's nothing to hope for now. That's why this place around here is a real and honest place. Do ye get me?'

I nodded.

'There's no plan any more. This is unprecedented. There is no father. There is no appeal. And hell, hell assumes its true fuckin significance. We're already there. I saw all this so fuckin clearly, durin a mushroom trip out here, one of the first times I came to this place. The mushrooms are like a technology, they let ye see what's happened to the world. Death is in everything now. I sat there cryin and screamin for hours. The entire sky was crushin me, all of outer space was pressin down on me, I was buried and I've never come back. I'm still buried. There is no surface, nowhere to claw back to. You're buried too, and ye know it, I can see it in ye. There is no father. There is no therapy. Do ye know how that feels?'

He watched me again, studying the effect of his words. He desperately wanted me to be awed. Despising myself, I pursed my lips and nodded, as if to say it was a profound insight he had just shared. I didn't know what else to do.

Maybe I had failed to mask my insincerity. 'What's your story?' he asked, guardedly, the portentous tone gone from his voice. Again I had the sense that the question was only a mimicking of curiosity. I said I was a college student but I'd dropped out, I was living at home now, I used to work as a security guard. I didn't mention the other stuff, the counsellors and psychiatrists.

'I used to be a security guard as well. Out here.' He gestured across the expanse. 'In a warehouse for computer parts. It was like guardin a new race. That was the last job I had. Fifteen years ago, it was. They fired me because I was useless and weak.'

I drank my can and we lingered in silence. I wondered what he had done in the fifteen years since losing his job. The light and warmth were seeping out of the day. Even in the quiet I could feel the intensity of the man's sidelong focus on me, the restless calculations as to how he could render himself fascinating and enigmatic in my eyes. I felt even lonelier, more famished and dejected in his presence than I felt on my own.

'This is where ye can be near to death,' he said. 'That's why I come here, to get the feel of me own death, to be waitin for it.'

I craved to vanish into the air. This was a man beyond salvage, doomed, but not in any romantic way; he was merely pathetic, shattered. I saw in him a vision of my own future.

I said I had to go.

'Sure I might see ye around here again,' he said quickly. 'I come out here a lot now.'

I muttered that yeah, maybe I would see him. Then I made my way out of the darkening estate, utterly silent now that the workers had left for the day. I walked out to the Long Mile Road and took a bus back home.

After that I didn't go to Ballymount for several days. Instead I stayed in the house, lying in bed or playing the Xbox, or I walked into town along the canal. On a cold and sunny afternoon I went to see a film in the IFI. The cinema was nearly empty. It was a film about a middle-aged man in the American Midwest whose son is in a coma, having shot himself in the head in a failed suicide attempt. One morning, at breakfast, the man looks at his wife for a long time, silently, not seeming to hear her questions and pleas. He stands up. Then he walks out of the house, and keeps on walking. He reaches the highway and begins to hitchhike north, crossing state lines, listening to the sad, broken or ecstatic people who pick him up, but saying little. He crosses the Canadian border. He slants across to the east. He walks to the ends of the roads, and keeps walking, out on to the bare and rocky coast, away from all human settlements. He reaches the Atlantic, cold and hissing, foaming over the rocks. He stops. He stands there and gazes out at the ocean, alone for miles around. Then he begins to laugh, a deep, resounding laugh, the first instance of joy he has shown in the film – but when we see his face, it is clear that there is no real joy, only the cold pretence of it. Then the camera slowly retreats, at an angle and into the sky, leaving us with a view of the man standing on the rocky outcropping. As the camera soars away he dwindles into pinprick insignificance, as if whatever meaning his story had is now dissolved in the infinite. The view of the coast and the ocean is hazed by wisping cloud. The screen is filled with white, the film ends.

The day after I had been to the cinema, I went back to the Ballymount estate. It was a cold, dreary afternoon; winter was approaching. Though I walked for more than four hours that day, I didn't see the man I had spoken with. When I came back again the next day, after wandering for an hour or so, I saw him sitting on the ground with a bag of cans by his side. He looked up as I approached. He didn't seem surprised; I wondered if this was an affectation. He offered me a can and I sat by him. A lone bird swooped down nearby, squawking before flying off again. It was evening now, a reddish burning sunset hazed with pollution. I knew what was coming: he would tell me his story. I knew he had been thinking of me since we had first met; not in or for myself, but as an instrument of his own self-recognition.

He drank deep from his can.

He told me:

He had been fostered by a widow, a very strict Catholic. He had never known his parents, or why they had put him up for adoption. He had always been the weirdo, the victim, the figure of ridicule at school. He remembered having his head shoved into a toilet full of shit. He had no memory of ever being happy. As a child he hated summer, the outdoors, and the passing of time, which was famished and blank. He went to art college, hoping to be recognized, to shine and be loved. But at a student house party he took two tabs of acid and he saw in a shock of total insight that here, too, he had always been the figure of ridicule, the one they lampooned and despised and jeered at behind his back; he recalled a thousand things they'd said to him, and only now did he see, in awful hindsight, the suppressed sneers and the mockery in their faces, all of them deceiving him, then howling with laughter when he turned away. From that night on, he was broken. The horror of realizing, in one blinding instant, the immense gulf between his grandiose perception of himself and how the others *really* saw him, shattered what was left of his self into fragments. His misery became so convoluted, dense and total as to be incommunicable. He lost his voice; he literally couldn't speak, because having a voice meant having a self, or a sense of self, some fundamental core of positive self-regard, and he didn't have that. He became totally impotent, unable even to masturbate. Incapable of functioning, he dropped out of college and retreated from the world, fled further and further into the fogged maze of himself until it had become impossible to find his way back out. For years he thought constantly of killing himself, and now believed that it was only the religious terrors instilled in him by his foster mother that had held him back. He lived on the dole and tried to convince himself that he was a great artist, that this was his season in hell, the terrible suffering that would give birth to the works that would redeem him, and eventually all the world would see what he had always been, and he would forgive them and he would be loved. He met an old schoolmate of his, an electronic-music producer who rented a dilapidated house in a secluded clearing off the Naas Road. He moved in with his old schoolmate and they lived together for several years. Then, one weekend while his friend was away, he burned the house to the ground. He could not say whether he had done this accidentally or on purpose. He stood outside, watching the house go up in flames, terrified and elated. He heard sirens in the distance and he fled. For several weeks he slept rough around Dublin, in parks, in alleys, by the canals, in corners of building sites and wastegrounds. At a school in Drimnagh he slept for a week in the playground, under the slide. One morning he was woken by the rough hands of two policemen under his arms, hauling him to his feet. They took him in and a day later he was admitted to St Patrick's mental hospital. He was prescribed medication and assigned a counsellor. After several months he was moved to an outpatients' home and allowed to come and go as he pleased. That was four years ago. He was still living there, receiving a steady welfare income, enough to buy cigarettes, cans and, occasionally, magic mushrooms. He never saw his friend who had taken him in and encouraged his painting. He never saw anyone. He just came to Ballymount to be alone with his thinking. He was thirty-nine years old, he said, and his destiny was to become a saint. My Lord is fire, and the Lord is coming.

His story drew to a close and now he watched me. When I left, he would be nothing but a swirl of visions, pain and memories. For now, I was a mirror in which he could almost convince himself that he was whole.

He rolled a cigarette and puffed hungrily on it. He drained a can and crumpled it in his bony hand. The night was coming on. What if the days keep on getting shorter, I thought, until there is only night?

'Listen,' he said, 'I can tell you're an intelligent fella. There are some other things, different things I want to tell ye. Ye look like you're able to handle big ideas. Will ye meet me here tomorrow? I'll show ye some of the weirder places.'

I nodded, wanting only to get away. Then I left him there, smoking and drinking in the wasteland as the night swarmed in to swallow him up. There is no therapy. There is no father. That night I dreamed, and in the dream I was back out there, on the estate. In the dream it went on for ever, the estate was the world and beyond it there was nothing. It was a dull afternoon. I saw him on the horizon, silhouetted and still. I walked towards him. Neither of us looked at the other, our eyes to the ground. 'Look at my burn marks,' he called out. 'And look at the slits. The Gestapo did this. CIA. Mujahedin. God is great. No one leaves the zone.' I looked up and we looked into each other's eyes. 'Beyond the horizon, a row of severed heads on sticks. Wooden chimes clicking in the wind.' And then there were no longer two of us, but one, we were together, he had come into me and now my fingernails were yellow and caked with dirt, and my clothes as I walked away, towards a lost road, were greyed and faded, my hair was thin and streaked, lifeless. I woke up sobbing, drenching the pillow with tears that streamed out of me like never before or since, pierced with a desolation I knew to be incurable, a condition I would carry with me for ever. I rose from the bed, feeling my way through the dark. I found my way to my mother's bedroom and turned the handle on the door. I heard her gasp in the dark. 'Don't worry,' I said. 'Go back to sleep. I'm sorry. Just let me lie beside your bed. I'm sorry. It's OK, I just need to lie here on the floor, just like this.' I could hear her hesitating, wanting to get up and fix this, but it couldn't be fixed and she lay back down. I knew she was staring upwards into the dark, her face gaunt with worry. After a while she got up and draped some covers over me, then got back into bed. I closed my eyes and tried to hear her breathing.

In the morning when I awoke, my mother was downstairs, cooking breakfast. I could smell coffee and frying bacon. A bird was chirping outside the window and beams of filtered sunlight warmed the room. I got up from the floor and went downstairs. My mother was sipping tea. She handed me a small, round cup, the one with a delicate Japanese sketch of a bird on the side. I could tell by her eyes that she had been crying and had slept badly, if at all, but she made an effort to smile. I smiled back. I put a hand on her shoulder. 'I'm goin to talk to them at the college,' I said. 'I'm goin to see if they'll take me back after Christmas. Ye never know, it might be worth a try.'

Peering at me with widened eyes over the curve of her teacup, my mother nodded faintly. She hesitated, fearful of crushed hopes. Then she said, 'I knew ye would. I never stopped prayin for ye.' Tears welled up, her voice was cracking. 'I never will stop prayin for ye. I mean it. I never will.'

Exiled in the Infinite – Killian Turner, Ireland's Vanished Literary Outlaw

It is impossible today to read either the work or the life of the novelist, essayist, epigrammatist and pornographer Killian Turner, without seeking in it clues to the mystery of his disappearance, or attempting to locate the genesis of the strange obsessions that would eventually consume him.

There is little beyond what Turner called 'the crash-landing site of my birthplace' by which he could meaningfully be called an 'Irish writer'. In fact, his body of work, taken as a whole, might be seen as Turner's lifelong project of effacing all marks of nationhood from his authorial voice and literary being. It is clear from comments made by Turner in his letters to other writers and artists (the majority of them obscure), and certain remarks in his essays,[1] that, like such pointedly

---

1. For instance: 'Why should it be that, in an age of burgeoning communication technologies which render geographical space increasingly insignificant,

un-Irish compatriot-predecessors as Beckett and Joyce, Turner wished to be considered first and foremost a European author.[2]

Born into an upper middle class family in Dalkey, County Dublin, in 1948, Turner only began writing with any seriousness in his early twenties.[3] It may be that Turner was prevented from writing as a younger man by the unhappiness of his home life. Maureen Turner, Killian's mother, died after complications resulting from the birth of her only child. Killian's father, Henry, was a history teacher in a private secondary school in Dalkey, and a man of trenchantly

---

a writer, or any artist, must continue to be categorised primarily in reference to his *national* peers and forebears? It is obvious to me that ... writers should henceforth be categorised according to affinities of style, areas of enquiry and formal concerns, rather than by the comparatively inexpressive fact of their birth-proximity to other writers.' (*Erased Horizons, Forgotten Shores: Essays 1975–1982*, Sacrum Press, Dublin).

2. Turner's gradual shedding of his national identity undoubtedly had a stimulating effect on the development of his art. Shorn of the parochial concerns which predominate in the work of many Irish writers of his generation, Turner was freed to soar far from the homeland, towards universal or exotic themes. In a famous essay, Jorge Luis Borges expresses frustration at Argentinian authors' unreflecting attachment to *place* in their work; seeing themselves primarily as Argentinian writers, they crowd their stories with local colour and content that caters to the literary sightseer and tourist. Yet why, asks Borges, should an Argentinian writer not eschew the constraining tropes of locational realism, and take as his subject the universe itself? Just as Borges met his own challenge, revolutionising the short story by engineering sublimely playful, metaphysical mysteries and ingenious hoax-narratives, so too did Killian Turner explode prejudices about what 'Irish literature' was allowed to do, grappling as he did with ideas of reckless scope and ambition: time, infinity, chaos, Nazism, nuclear war, sex, evil and language itself (conceived, via Burroughs, as a relentless viral weapon, of origin foul but obscure).

3. At twenty-four he published his first short story, in a Trinity College journal. 'Father Coward' is the confessional monologue of a north Dublin priest who secretly harbours heretical notions concerning the true, chilling significance of the visions at Fatima.

melancholy disposition. In the smog-choked winter evenings of Killian's boyhood and adolescence, Henry would call his son into his study. There, as Killian stood silently by his side, the father would issue sweeping utterances about the destruction inherent in the very cells of civilization, the transience of mankind, and the utter folly of all our humanistic dreams of progress, peace and salvation. The cold gaze of scientific comprehension, declared father to son, betrays the appalling truth of our place in the universe as an accidental and fear-crazed species, rubbing its bleary eyes to find itself perched aboard a rock that hurtles through black infinities, whose only destiny is to be swallowed up once more in the great darkness. Religion, morality, truth, human solidarity – these are nothing, proclaimed the father, but the consoling fictions bred by our proximity to the abyss and the panic it engenders.

It can only be imagined what impression these dark lessons had on the sensitive young Killian. What we can be sure of, however, is that the great, seismic event of Turner's youth was the suicide by poisoning of Henry Turner at the age of fifty-three, when Killian was eighteen. This event, reappearing in various guises, is the black hole, the vortex of destructive fury around which Turner's writing orbits, drawing ever closer, inviting – and this is what gives the experience of reading Turner what has been called its 'vertiginous', 'abyssal' quality – a kind of cosmic-orgasmic catastrophe in the psyche of both reader and writer.

Until the death of his father, Turner seems to have been a rather normal child and young man. He enjoyed hurling, soccer and Gaelic football. His schoolmates and friends remembered him as being quiet, but devastatingly witty when called upon to use his wit as a weapon, and gently hilarious when among friendlier company. He was something of a loner by disposition, yet not unpopular. Beginning in early child-hood, Turner read voraciously. In his teens he had a colossal appetite for science fiction and so-called 'weird' fiction. (His fascination with the work of H.P. Lovecraft bordered on the religious: the young Turner would spend whole weekends in his room, drawing wildly imaginative pictures of the Old Ones of Lovecraftian mythology. Not infrequently, his father and any visitors to the household would be startled by sudden, bellowed recitals, issuing from Killian's bedroom, of the incantations of savage tribes to their hellish gods familiar to readers of Lovecraft's stories: *Ph'nglui mglw'nafh Cthulhu R'lyeh wgah'nagl fhtagn!*)

In his late teens and early twenties, Turner lived on the inheritance he had received upon his father's death. He did not pursue third-level studies, though he did continue to read as much, and more widely than ever, nourishing keen inter-ests in mythology, anthropology and avant-garde physics. It was during this period that Turner began to imagine he could become a writer. At the age of twenty-five, having published two short stories and several reviews in various Irish jour-nals and newspapers, he set to work on his first novel. *Edge of Voices* took four years to complete, and a further two to find a publisher, finally seeing print when its author was thirty-one. Regarded from its first appearance as one of the true oddities of Irish literature (a literature hardly scarce of oddities), the novel is equal parts semi-autobiographical portrayal of an unremarkable Dublin adolescence, and fantas-tical, eerie missive from the furthermost extremes of human experience. The story, such as it is, tells of a boy, Michael Kavanagh, similar in most ways to Turner, who, on the day of his Catholic confirmation, begins to receive, or believe he is receiving, telepathic messages from a hyper-intelligent presence, perhaps extraterrestrial or inter-dimensional in origin, which may once have inhabited the earth in corporeal form, but now exists only as an imperceptible atmospheric layer. Michael is deeply troubled by the messages, often doubting his own sanity. Yet he continues to live his outward life more or less as usual, enduring the timeless trials of adolescence and winning local renown as a full-back on the under-17 Gaelic football team. Then, after Michael reaches his eighteenth birthday, loses his virginity (in what must rank as one of the most hilarious love scenes in Irish fiction) and applies to study European History at Trinity College, all in the same bittersweet week, the transmissions abruptly cease, never to resume. The final sixty pages of the book are given over to an exegesis, supposedly set down in the fourth millennium AD, of the messages received by Michael over a three-year period during his adolescence. The implication seems to be that Michael has become some sort of messiah, or the founder of a new religion or civilization.

Edge of Voices was first published not in Ireland but in France, and then in New York, by small independent presses committed to the literary heterodox. Turner gave several readings in Paris, where he gained minor cult status. Then, when he was thirty-three, he received an Irish Arts Council bursary, which he used to fund a trip around Europe. He travelled for three months, filling several notebooks with reflections on post-war Europe that were to inform his work for years to come. Instead of returning to Ireland after his travels, Turner settled in West Berlin, where he was to remain for the final three years prior to his disappearance.

Throughout the early eighties, from the anarchist and bohemian neighbourhood of Friedrichshain he had made his home, Turner continued to send stories, essays and other, increasingly uncategorisable writings almost exclusively to Irish journals, as if still engaged in a dialogue with a land he had otherwise repudiated. (By no means were all of these pieces accepted for publication.) Turner rented a small apartment in a block largely occupied by political radicals and artists, and seemed to thrive in this environment. The poet Sarah Flanagan, who also lived in Berlin around this time and befriended Turner, later remarked that his apartment had something of the monk's cell to it. 'There was a stove, a pot, a pan, a few cups and plates, a desk, and a bed. Apart from that, the only things he had were books,' she said. Asked about Turner's social and romantic life in this period, she replied: 'I don't know what to say about that. I mean, for sure he was handsome, and he had a certain charisma. But there was a ... a kind of privacy to him that went beyond simple introspectiveness. Like he would only let you come so far, and then he'd step out into the grounds of the castle to meet with you. He was never unfriendly, never cold. But there was a boundary. I used to wonder about his love life. He never told me about it, and when I asked he was always wittily evasive. Later, of course, there were all the rumours, but I didn't know him any more by that stage ... I used to tell him he looked like Michel Foucault, with the bald head, the intense eyes, the glasses. He liked that. He rarely laughed, but he had a lively, faint kind of smile. I remember that.'

Living within sight of the Berlin Wall, steeped in the atmosphere of what he called 'the city on earth that has come closest to the core of the darkness, hearing the very beat of the devil's wing', Turner's lifelong fascination with Nazi Germany, the Holocaust and the Second World War found endless stimulation. He took long, aimless walks through the city, at all times of day or night, overcome with visions of the enormity that had been perpetrated there mere decades ago. Reading deeply from the literature of the war, Turner developed what he described as a 'merciless obsession' with Hitler's plan, devised during the height of the Third Reich's reach and ambition, to convert the island of Ireland into the 'granary of Europe' following the final triumph of Nazism. Turner's second book, *The Garden*, was the controversial fruit of this obsession.

Coining the term 'Nazi-pastoral' to describe an almost aggressively uncategorisable work, critics were not quite sure how seriously to take its plotless, meticulously realized, deadpan portrait of an alternative, Nazified Ireland in which Hitler's plan has come to pass. Written in a documentary style recalling sociological surveys and governmental reports, *The Garden* was, according to one critic, 'either a joke in questionable taste, or the nostalgic, vindictive fantasy of a confused and lonely man, whose bitterness has bred a disingenuous sympathy for the Nazis and for Hitler'. Indeed, defenders of the book, who insisted it was an extended exercise in cautionary irony, foundered when they tried to explain away the all-too-convincing sincerity in Turner's depictions of a bucolic Ireland run by communities of agrarian fascists, where cheery colleens Irish-dance around swastikas, and boys in the Hitler Youth of Ireland (whose honorary president is W.B. Yeats) are taught to hunt, cook and swim, whilst having their imaginations fed by Celtic and Nordic mythology, and receiving lessons in the rudiments of Darwinism and race theory.

Thus far, sexuality had had a somewhat muted presence in Turner's work. Turner himself appears to have always been at ease with his own homosexuality (or strong homosexual tendencies), even if he was reluctant to publicise it in the conservatively Catholic Ireland where he had come of age. In Berlin, however, Turner took full advantage of the city's fierce permissiveness to explore this sexuality in a deeper way than had been possible hitherto. The discoveries he made in the course of these explorations, based on his writings subsequent to *The Garden*, were strange and disturbing, hinting at the darkest recesses of the Sadean imagination. 'It was as if', writes one of Turner's most perceptive and sympathetic critics, '[he] came to view his sexuality, and beyond that, the broader configuration of his instinctual drives, as a kind of map or diagram in which he could discern, in microcosm, all the horrors and psychopathology – political, social, personal – of the traumatic century into which he had been born.'[4]

Abandoning the last vestiges of conventional narrative fiction, and taking as his new literary models Bataille,[5] Sade and Burroughs, Turner ventured into murky, often questionable artistic territories. At the same time, and with equal conviction, he conducted countless nocturnal forays into Berlin's transgressive, erotic underworld. His most grotesque or bizarre adventures found their way into the writings of this period – writings which convey the unholy, anarchic allure of the Berlin night, in pages crowded with masochistic dog-men, dungeon-crawling 'spiritual abortions', bald women draped in chains 'with vaginas in their armpits and armpits in their

---

4. Thomas Duddy, 'Bludgeoning the Muse – the Transgressive Anti-Fiction of Killian Turner', *Review of Contemporary Literature*, Issue 68, June 2002.

5. For a period, Turner even seems to have entertained the belief that he himself was the reincarnation of Bataille: 'Not figuratively, but in the full meaning of spirit recast, power enfleshed ... There are nights when, woken by the howl of a junkie down in Boxhagener Strasse or the rattle of a late U-Bahn train, I walk to the darkened mirror, and from it peer the radiant, saintly eyes of Georges Bataille.' (*Visions of Cosmic Squalor/The Upheaval*, Anti-Matter, London.) However, as Bataille lived until 1962, and was therefore Turner's contemporary for fourteen years, it is difficult to understand how Turner even considered holding this eccentric notion.

vaginas', weeping teenage prostitutes from the Soviet hinterlands, and mute rent-boys with pure and sorrowful visages.

By this time, Turner had learned German well enough to hold a series of unglamorous jobs in Berlin (he was not making nearly enough from his writing to live on). He worked for a spell as a night-watchman on building sites on the fringes of the city. Then he got a job as a caterer on trains connecting West Berlin to various cities to the north. In one of his most difficult passages, Turner writes of the strange happiness he experienced in this job, peering out the windows at 'the silent dream of passing German landscape, a sublimely dreary post-industrial idyll whose every inch sang of holocaust – of the holocaust already passed and the holocausts to come, for all infinity, an eternal recurrence of this most perfect human exaltation and nightmare, the ecstatic vision of an engineered hell ... And then I would interrupt my window-gazing reveries and, suffused with a world-embracing love like that described by the mystics, serve Coca-Cola, orange juice and ham sandwiches to beautiful German children and their waddling parents.'[6]

---

6. Admittedly, while all of the late Turner is challenging, some of the fragmentary work of his final years, especially certain of the pieces collected in *Visions of Cosmic Squalor/The Upheaval*, can only be described as unhinged. And yet, even the most aberrant of his work has a quality of dazzling entertainment. Consider the sprawling, unfinished essay, worked on during the early eighties and unpublished at the time of his disappearance, in which Turner asserts that Joyce's final novel, the monstrous *Finnegans Wake*, is nothing less than a coded transmission intended to trigger the apocalypse. According to Turner (and this has been ridiculed by the few scholars who have bothered to address the issue at all), while Joyce was living in Trieste, he was contacted by a sinister group of Cabbalistic Jews who, given impetus by the events of the First World War, were promulgating an eschatological doctrine in which language itself figured as a kind of super-weapon, radiating metaphysical contaminants through the media of literature, radio and cinema. Joyce, writes Turner, most likely considered the

It is at this point that a heavier fog descends on the biographical trail; fact, fiction and hallucination become impossible to separate. Most of what follows cannot be verified as factual truth, having been pieced together from Turner's perilous later writings and the sparse accounts of those who knew him at the time. It is entirely possible that most of what is here recounted bears no relation to events that took place in external reality. However, it is the author's belief that what follows is, at least, an approximation of the reality that pertained within the troubled psyche of Killian Turner in the period leading to the autumn of 1985. The only events which undoubtedly did take place are those of Turner's disappearance and the subsequent investigation; the rest must be considered either metaphor or speculation.

In November or December of 1984, Turner agreed to collaborate on an industrial-noise track with a musician friend, Heinrich Mannheim, who he knew through the S/M underworld. Mannheim's band, Sublime Ascent, was at the extreme end of the thriving noise-music scene in Berlin in the eighties. They took their cue from bands like Whitehouse, whose aesthetic of extreme violence and sexual cruelty Mannheim considered the only cultural form immune to assimilation by the capitalist-consumer system. Sublime Ascent are reported to have incorporated images and video footage of war atrocities, executions and torture into their infrequent live shows. It has even been rumoured that, in one extremely secretive performance in a disused governmental premises on the

conspiring Cabbalists as nothing more than a picturesque nuisance. However, he goes on, the Cabbalists submitted an unwitting Joyce to a refined form of hypnotism, implanting him with the apocalyptic codes, syntactic rhythms and linguistic motifs which their ancient studies had revealed to them as the ammunition of cosmic disarray – and which, according to Turner, were to surface, unbeknownst to Joyce, across the expansive tapestry of his most mystifying novel.

fringes of either Frankfurt or Dresden, the band improvised a set to the prolonged, ritualistic killing of a consenting and ecstatic male, hands bound and on his knees, a series of cuts made on his naked torso.

The tapes said to have resulted from the collaboration between Sublime Ascent and Killian Turner have become the holy grail of Turner aficionados. On the recordings, Turner is thought to have read from a collage made up of his own texts and those of Georges Bataille, possibly spliced with certain passages from Sade and Nietzsche, and transcripts of the commentary from the 1982 World Cup. He read over a sprawling sound-texture that lurched between extreme noise and eerie, dark-ambient sonic wasteland, performed live by Sublime Ascent. Present at the recording was a forty-something man with long, greying hair and a bushy, black moustache who was never to be seen without his wraparound sunglasses, his overall appearance suggesting a somewhat seedier Carlos Santana. This was the figure Turner would refer to in his writings sometimes as Frank Lonely, but more often as Mother D. After watching the recording session whilst drinking several cups of herbal tea, Frank Lonely/Mother D remarked that he admired the text which Turner had read, or at least what he had understood of it (his English was imperfect), and thought he had recognized certain phrases from Georges Bataille. When the day's recording was finished, the two men went out for a drink and ended up talking long into the night – about art, music, love and politics. Turner eventually stumbled back to his Friedrichshain apartment as a murky dawn broke over Berlin, rarely in his life having laughed or enjoyed himself so much.

The diaries Turner kept in the months immediately preceding his disappearance detail his intense, at times all-consuming friendship with Mother D. The two men shared a love for Bataille, for underground American rock bands like Suicide and Big Black, and, bizarrely, for most varieties of animated film, but especially those produced by the Disney corporation. Turner and Mother D would spend their week-ends visiting cinemas all over the city, watching *Bambi*, *The Jungle Book*, *Snow White and the Seven Dwarfs*, and what-ever other feature-length cartoons they could find (they appear to have had no interest in shorter fare, such as animated TV series). 'In the presence of Mother D I re-embody the child I never truly was,' wrote Turner, 'which in turn prepares me, spiritually if not fizzically [sic] for what is to come, i.e. the great radiance/the crossing/the sacred blah-blah-blah.'[7]

It was towards the end of July that Mother D introduced Turner to a friend and ex-lover of his named Anashka. Turner was instantly enthralled. Indeed, Anashka seems to have been a formidable figure, of no great beauty, perhaps, but with intense erotic allure. Born to a Russian mother in exile from the Soviet Union, and an Italian anarchist father, Anashka always wore a black beret and tight black jeans, though the rest of her apparel varied wildly. 'The beret and jeans were the frame,' wrote Turner. 'The rest was the whir-ring reel ... of a film I could watch for ever.' Anashka was twenty-nine and co-ran a gallery and performance space in Lichtenberg. She was also an artist who used the medium of dance, often augmented with vitriolic spoken-word outbursts and even, when the chemistry of a performance demanded it, physical assaults on her audience. One night

---

7. A certain lightness of tone, unusual in Turner's work, can be detected in passages and diary entries written during these months, as if the happiness inspired by his friendship with Mother D could not but seep through into Turner's authorial voice.

she performed to an audience consisting solely of Turner, in an apartment borrowed from a friend who was visiting Poland. Turner was transfixed by the dance, which consisted for the most part of Anashka standing deathly still, wincing very occasionally, and emitting long, alarming shrieks even more infrequently. After almost three hours, Anashka collapsed to the floor and announced that the performance had concluded. Turner thanked her and asked her what the piece was called. Anashka thought about this for quite some time, before replying, *Jack Ruby and Lee Harvey Oswald.* Turner and Anashka then made love on the floor of the apartment – an experience which astonished Turner. He was to write at length about this incident on several occasions, as if trying to coax out its core meaning by approaching it from multiple angles. 'I cannot say', he concluded, 'whether the carnal fusion with Anashka was the greatest bliss of my life ... or the deepest horror.'

The day after Anashka's performance, Mother D told Turner of an abandoned house in the countryside just outside Berlin, in the shadow of an Autobahn flyover. For months, he and Anashka had been talking about taking over the house and turning it into some kind of art space or music studio. Though nothing came of this intention, Mother D did drive Turner out to the house one unusually cold afternoon in early September. For Turner, whose mental state was most likely entering a stage of extreme deterioration, visiting the house was an experience of near-religious intensity. He had the sense of being in a place that existed outside of time, a primal, sacred and abyssal site, a 'portal on to infinity', where 'good and evil are one, are nothing'. While it is not clear whether Turner continued to visit the house after Mother D had revealed its location to him, his writing immediately became fixated on the image of a dilapidated house, unoccupied, on the fringes of a vast post-industrial city. In what has become unofficially known as the House Sequence, written in a frenzy of productivity throughout that September, the structure is described as having cracked walls and smashed windows, and is overrun with weeds, yet radiates an intense, unearthly beauty. Across a broody strip of wasteland from the house, the broad, silent Autobahn soars indifferently past, 'like mighty Quetzalcoatl'. In the opening variations of the sequence, the house stands serenely abandoned, crumbling and unwitnessed. Later, as the sequence gathers 'a kind of entropic momentum',[8] Turner begins to introduce human presences into the scene. One, two or, at most, three figures appear, always in the middle of the afternoon. They enter the house through the side or back door, which creaks on its hinges, and walk silently through the dilapidation. Various images occur and dissolve: a couple mutedly make love on the dusty floor; a man hangs a painting on a cracked, bare wall and gazes at it for hours, tears running down his face (we never see what the picture represents); a solitary woman, clearly modelled on Anashka, enters a bedroom and lies on the damp floorboards where a bed might once have been. She lies there for a long time, gazing at the ceiling. She begins to masturbate, but stops before reaching orgasm. Darkness falls and still the woman has not moved. Suddenly we see her as a skeleton.

In the penultimate variation in the sequence, the house is the setting of a suicide. On a melancholy afternoon in autumn, a woman and a naked man watch in silence as a second man slits his wrists in the overgrown back garden. His

8. Thomas Duddy, 'Ecstatic Slaughter: Human Sacrifice in the Work of Georges Bataille and Killian Turner', *Radical Philosophy*, Issue 116, Winter 1999.

body slumps to the ground and the man and woman stare at it for a long time (the moon rises, falls; the sun rises, falls). Then they leave. Finally, in what is both the termination of the House Sequence and the last of Killian Turner's known writings, a man arrives at the house, alone, holding a pile of photographs. He spends the night walking from room to room, weeping occasionally. In each room he stops and looks at some of the photographs, sometimes letting one fall to the floor, or placing one on a mantelpiece or windowsill. Very early in the morning, he leaves the house, gets into a red car which he has parked nearby, and drives away. The car merges with the Autobahn that soars out and away from the city, towards an unknowable horizon.

The House Sequence was posted to Turner's publishers in mid-October. Near the end of that month, Killian Turner was reported as missing by his landlord. His rent had been due for three weeks. His apartment bore no suggestion that Turner had fled – the cupboard was reasonably well-stocked and his personal belongings had not been removed. The West Berlin authorities interviewed acquaintances of Turner, along with residents of his apartment block. No one could say where he had gone, nor did they know of any friends or family of Turner's who might be contacted in Ireland. After an examination of the diaries and notebooks found in his apartment, efforts were made to trace the individuals referred to as Mother D/Frank Lonely and Anashka. However, none of Turner's acquaintances were able to identify either of these from the descriptions given by the authorities. It appears that those involved in investigating Turner's disappearance reached the conclusion that neither Mother D nor Anashka really existed. Eventually, when several months had passed and nothing came up in the case, Killian Turner was officially declared a missing person by the West German authorities, and the whole affair was quickly forgotten.

Today, Killian Turner is remembered and read by but a few scattered devotees to the literature of collapse. Perhaps this is a fitting destiny for the man who declared, in a typically self-consuming aphorism, 'It is not enough to court extinction; *our* aspiration is *never to have been.*'

Paris Story

It happens like this. While living in Paris, X writes a novel based on his experiences as an expat. The novel receives interest from several publishers, but none of them is finally willing to take it on. Meanwhile, X's friend K, who is also living in Paris, completes her first collection of short stories. K is signed up by a literary agent and, within a month, the collection is sold to a major publisher.

While X has always been encouraging of K's writing, in private he considers it sentimental storytelling, of no great literary moment. X begins working on another novel, but progress is slow and difficult. Meanwhile, K's collection is published and is an immediate success. K begins appearing in newspapers and on radio shows. X and K still meet for coffee, or drink in wine bars with their friends, and take walks in the Jardin du Luxembourg. While they walk, K admits to X how pleasant it is to receive the media attention, yet ultimately how silly and inconsequential. Maybe, maybe not, thinks X.

X plunges on with his new novel. It is set partly during the French-Algerian war (he has stacks of books borrowed from the library), and partly in contemporary Paris, among expat writers like himself and K. In short, it is a more ambitious novel than his first. He soon feels overwhelmed: he has lost the thread; the novel is a chaos of interminable sentences and scenes with no clear connection to one another.

In an interview with an expat magazine, K mentions X. She refers to him as a 'writer of real ambition, one to watch out for'. Initially, X is flattered. Soon, however, he feels only anger and disgust. It is clear to him: K now considers X to be beneath her. One evening, after a long walk from the eleventh arrondissement to the rue de l'Odéon and back again, X sits down at his desk and writes about K's story collection. He pours all the bile and scorn that have been festering inside him on to the page. At first, he is writing the piece only for himself. By the time he has composed the final paragraph, though, he knows he will have it published.

The review is accepted by a well-known literary website. X publishes it under a pseudonym – J. Curtis. It is K's first experience of a truly hostile review. She stays at home for two days. At the end of the second day, she calls X and talks quietly about the review for several minutes, then begins to cry. X feels uncomfortable – by now, he regrets publishing the piece and knows that, if K ever finds out who its true author is, their friendship will be over. Please come, K says. X feels he cannot say no.

On the way to K's apartment on rue Moret, X buys a bottle of wine. They drink this together, listening to Nina Simone. Though neither of them mentions the review for almost an hour, X can see the effect it has had on K – she looks as if she has the flu. Abruptly, K opens her laptop and reads aloud some of the harshest sentences. X says nothing. Then K shuts the laptop and says, Let's go out and get drunk. They drink red wine in a bar on the Quai de Jemmapes, by the canal. A band plays jazz. X stares at the double bass player, a young man with a tormented expression who seems somehow familiar (for years afterwards, X will be haunted by his face). That night, X and K end up in bed together. Though this is not something that either of them has ever particularly longed for, both find it satisfying. In the morning, K stays in bed while X makes coffee, then goes out and buys pastries and croissants from the patisserie on the corner. After breakfast, they make love again. X feels an urge to confess that it was he who wrote the hostile review. He suppresses the urge.

From that morning on, X and K spend many hours each day in one another's company. They write together through the afternoons, and see their friends in the evenings. X even begins to find a way back into his novel. In short, they are enjoying an idyll. However, X burns with guilt for the brutal review he published of K's collection. He no longer even agrees with the arguments he levelled against her, though he knows they were of a sophistry that will have convinced many.

Years pass. K and X have married and are now living in Dublin. K has written two more story collections and a novel. X's novel involving the French-Algerian war has also been published. X writes book reviews, and the couple manage to raise their young daughter solely on money earned through literary activity. One September, K leaves Ireland to give a talk at a conference in Munich, before spending three weeks at a writers' residency near Heidelberg. While she is gone, X receives a phone call. He picks up the receiver and hears nothing. Eventually, X curses the mute caller and hangs up.

Later that evening, X receives an email from an unfamiliar address. It says, *You are a liar*. The email is signed *J. Curtis*.

X is badly unnerved: it takes a third of a bottle of whiskey to calm him down. When he finally falls asleep on the couch with the television on, he dreams of the review he wrote years earlier of K's book. In the dream, naked men sit at their computers, reading the review while masturbating slowly. Later, the website is revealed to be embedded in a cliffside. The name of the website is 'Melted Face'.

The next day there is a second email. The message is repeated – *You are a liar* – and this time there is an address: 38 rue du Borrégo, Appartement 107, Paris. This is intolerable, X thinks. He decides that he must travel to Paris while K is abroad, and confront his accuser at the address indicated.

X flies out that Monday morning, having left his daughter with her grandparents. He spends the first afternoon wandering the districts where he had spent the happiest years of his vanished youth. After dinner that evening at a bistro near the Sorbonne, X decides to enter a small cinema where a film is about to start. He sits in a middle row, away from the few scattered viewers. In the film, a man in his sixties is living with his cat in an apartment in Brussels, shunning the world. One day, a young woman appears at his door. Various misunderstandings ensue, which result in the older man and the woman driving across Europe in a sports car. (X's French is rusty and the finer details of the plot escape him, though he believes it involves either an annulled marriage or an attempted kidnapping.) The film ends in Reims, where the woman draws a revolver and shoots a squat, bearded Asian man in a bowler hat, for reasons which remain opaque to X.

The following morning, X resolves to visit rue du Borrégo. He takes the Métro, and as he holds the overhead hand rail and watches the Parisians sharing his carriage, he imagines the paths both his and K's lives would have taken if K had learned, years ago, that he was the author of that cruel review. He disembarks from the Métro at Saint-Fargeau and follows the map on his phone, which takes him off the avenue, down a quiet street with high residential blocks on either side. When X reaches number 38, he presses the bell for apartment 107. There is no answer. An elderly woman exits the building and X lets himself in behind her. He ascends the poorly lit staircase until he reaches the top floor. He knocks on the door of 107. Nobody comes. He presses his ear against it, but can hear no sound from inside. He knocks forcefully, many times. He cries out, 'I'm here. Open up. Who's in there?' His voice resounds through the stairwell. Then X throws his weight against the door with his shoulder. To his surprise, it opens.

The apartment is bare and unfurnished. The walls, floor and ceiling are all of grey cement. There are no panes in the windows, and X can see the higher floors of the building across the street. A cold breeze blows through the apartment. X enters each room, but it is all the same. No one has ever lived here, he thinks. Fleetingly, it seems to X that he has been here many times. After standing in the middle of the largest room for a long time, he leaves the apartment.

That night, X gets extremely drunk in a series of ugly bars around Clichy. When he finally returns to his hotel, he falls into bed without undressing. His sleep is hot and jagged. As dawn filters greenly through the curtains, X dreams of K. In the dream, K's skin is pale and she never meets X's eyes. He tries to follow her head so he can look at her directly, but it swivels, always out of reach. Finally, her head separates from her body. Then K is gone, and the squat, bearded Asian man appears. He says to X, There is a man who has sucked your wife's nipples. When? asks X. In August, says the Asian man.

Outposts

1. *World Without End*

Afraid of all that lay ahead, she felt closer to him than ever. 'The time is past when man thought of himself in terms of a dawn.' They drive along the curving, shadowy streets. The shutters are already closed throughout town. The wind sweeps the church and its surroundings. 'An ache I soothed with prayers and codeine.' A car approaches. 'What if he asks for our names?' There were tears in her eyes.

*

The door opened. A grimy old woman in a headscarf. Everyone moves with deliberation. 'I don't understand it,' he says. 'Giving up is cowardly. So is carrying on.'

'Silence please.'

*

They are in bed, windows open to the morning coolness. Analysis of the passions, a definition of love. Faith, she thinks, is more mechanical than doubt. The wild light in her eyes. Or rather, almost wild.

'Great minds are very near to madness.'

*

A photograph on a mantelpiece: his future wife. The light was better then. 'Nature can hardly be forgiven.'

Goes over to the table where the American woman is sitting. 'In Barcelona I turned thirty.' 'Yes, I remember perfectly.' Slowly the light changes. Old surfaces of the town. They walk on to a balcony. 'It's hopeless.' 'This is what you wanted.' Season follows season, world without end. 'We have known each other for ever.' 'It isn't enough.'

*

I was alone, as if face to face with a blank rock. Traders and pedlars in the sunshine, the major marketplace. No one stands still under that dome, in dim shadows. 'If it smells like shit, it probably is.' I won't see her again, he thought. Spends her years making propaganda like someone stirring a burnt-out fire. She was more beautiful than –

In the morning, a little lucidity and few illusions left. Hotel melancholy. Now she goes out to the coast for the summer, in a caravan, where the estuary becomes tidal. A feeling of eternity. Black hair, an open window. It is already afternoon. The Volkhov River.

Asians wearing European labels. Hotels erected on the shore. A whale's skeleton at the base of a limestone cliff. The last race, all colour and fire. Instead of dreams, memories. 'I have returned to Europe and its struggles.' The Russian ballerinas, they dance very well. Red stone buildings, copper pagodas. The fragility of those shacks. 'They used to run this place like clockwork, but now …' The church square is rather sad. Love is possible, but unlikely. Young men with fine features and cold, knowing gazes. People who seek to be useful (not us, my love). 'A book is a postponed suicide,' mutters the tramp as he slumps in a doorway. Even in a large city, the streets at night are relatively still. How lonely it is to be alive.

*

In a Genoa hotel room, hears the ringing of bells resound through quiet streets at dusk. I leave the world as I found it.

This Is the Ritual

Face covered against the pollution, she fumbled in her bag for a coin. The entire ritual had been tainted. 'If I had children, I would strangle them here and now.'

Under a metallic sky, composing music far away from the war. Valiant but vain attempts to find a common language.

*

Sex detached from any genital processes. He goes back to bed and lies down. She is too old for him.

'Kiss me.'

'I never thought my mother would become my mistress.'

*

I was watching television on New Year's Eve. The demons were getting worse. ('It's a long trip. We are the only riders.')

*

When she arrived at the Greyhound station she understood that something was different. Sound of gunfire ... Funeral processions ... Atrocity footage in black and white ... 'This is the ritual.' She drinks coffee from a Styrofoam cup and looks over the crumpled sheet music, puts it away again.

*

Dusk, the lights of windows in high-rise blocks. 'Take me there.' A bullet shattered the pane in the lift. For a few days the girl seemed to lose her mind. 'You have to live your life, that's all there is to it.' Suddenly the voice of a human being becomes a towering edifice. 'I can't stand it any longer.' She turned to those who deny all taboos, all shame. 'Again and again I am engulfed by it.' She died miserably. Windy city outskirts.

*

I was drinking whiskey with two French friends. City outskirts. Smell of used condoms, excrement. Conversation revolved around sick dogs and a viable home. I thought of Claudel. (My erect cock seeking his testicles, his scrotum.) All my previous conditioning disqualifies me from what we face now. The city is a cemetery, the tramp used to say. Graffiti I saw in a Métro station: *I am come to destroy the works of women*. Realizing then that her fears were real.

I endure myself.

*

Nothing in his face reveals suicidal tendencies, she thinks. An advertisement for whiskey. The four provinces of Ireland. Flecks of snow in the sea air. They rarely speak. She has always associated sex with the sea. *Our Lady of the Dark Interstellar Spaces*.

Onward. Landscapes seen through train windows. No one is expecting to be thanked. 'I love your ferocity,' she says. Snow in the sea air. Windy city outskirts. 'Swear I will also be your victim.' Smell of condoms, excrement. They travel widely. A young male lover, known to pick pockets and carry a knife. Lost a fortune. As if from a distance, sadly but gently: 'The triumph of death and pain.'

*

The canteen was all but deserted. An elderly woman scribbling a mathematical equation. 'We live in a climate of exhaustion.' Outside the window the sky is darkening. Night after night I had passed these houses. 'There are bodies by the pool.' '*Non.*'

My salary ran out in Paris. 'I'm no longer capable of rage.' 'I'm still young, I need sex. It's normal.'

Late at night there would be older people at the tables, sometimes couples. Habit dulls intensity and marriage implies habit. 'That was just poetry.' Buses that don't arrive. A café that is closed for the summer.

'Needed you, Claudel.'

*

She fantasized about picking up a hitch-hiker. A couple of strangers, their faces seemed familiar. Windy city outskirts. Psychopaths preserved in a nature reserve. Unmade beds that smell of excrement. 'All the same she was a good-looking woman, in a common, feral way.'

*

She watched him with a faint, sceptical smile. He was sitting on the bed, drinking a beer. *There subsists in man a movement which always exceeds the bounds, that can only be partially reduced to order.* He lay down. She shook her head, a faraway gaze. *The transgressive side of marriage often escapes notice.*

'I never thought my mistress would become my mother.'

*

Long shadow of the corporation. In a late-night shop she buys a bottle of gin ... Scattered factions near the border ... That bar, always full of smoke and drunks … Late-evening sun … The estates … 'We must have a formula, if only to give a façade to the void.'

I leave the world as I found it.

2. *The Outer Sites*

We drive in silence. Fox eyes flash in the headlights and she curses under her breath. Corroded, like everything in our marriage. 'Answer me, you fucking bitch.' 'If you're going to do it, just fucking do it.' Moment of weakness, like many before. Both of us fantasise, both of us are tired. These streets are decomposing, he thinks drowsily. Cocktails at the weekend with the Herriots.

*

The orgasm came quickly, powerfully. A chubby boy in an anonymous hotel. Desert highway, far from any need for conversation. Not creating a life, not changing for anyone. I never said I was lost. Later, the boy stands in the moonlight like a god or a phantom. 'But you disappeared years ago!' Wind across the plains. In the distance a coyote whines. A man devoid of hope, with no investment in the future. 'No one lives for ever, therefore no one is alive.' 'A banal assertion.' Fires burn along the mountain.

*

They were watching him from across the table. Hard, ugly faces, missing teeth, utter lack of warmth or sympathy – no better than cannibals. 'Where is she?' 'Gone.' His teeth on edge like acrobats. Muttered curses, glances passed among them. They get up and leave the canteen. *Time of our dire need*. They found the old lady by an open window that night,

57

broken in various ways. Consign them all to the pits of hell.

Aren't you dead, like us? 'Only on the inside.'

*

The body had been riddled with bullets. 'He'll disappear, the way they all did.' 'People think it's revenge.' 'As if this had a logic.' A day of drizzle and wind. Headlights in the rain. (The Herriots? No, that other couple.) A lone eccentric, he lived in the woods. They say he ate magic mushrooms and sat out in the moonlight. Intense dialogues with unseen beings. Various other rumours, likewise unsavoury. Contact with outer reality was rare. He wrote poetry, such as this: 'Grant no peace to disturbed remains/Knowledge resides at the limit/Burnt-out ruins on the horizon, no place for a woman of breeding.' Lecherous half-thoughts: 'Her blood is streaming everywhere, flowing into my groin. Her beautiful ankles ... Lick me if you like me.' Energetic resolutions, guilt, resignation, etc.

*

Living on the island, she thought often of Jean-Paul. Not that she hadn't had lovers since. The longest day was past. Still, these visions of him asleep on the bed, naked ... Writes a book whose themes are betrayal, hatred, the lure of utter destruction. 'I was bored.' 'We're all fucking bored.' That Russian girl, no one would deny she was attractive, though in a fickle, plastic way. 'You destroyed what we had for *her*?' There's always some excuse, rarely a justification. One morning she had gone to a riding school where the trainer always eyed her hungrily – revenge was inevitable. But let a lost boy have his erotic moments, she thinks now. After all, we live in flames, it's better we are never truly known. Then: it's a free world, the twenty-first century. (Late-night film in her beach cabin:

orgasms real or fake, it's all the same to her. A couple drives in silence, headlights in the rainy dark. 'Just fucking do it.' 'I'll *never* take you back!' 'Suit yourself, like you always do.')

*

Natalya rides a train to the peripheries. For love of this world, she pledges calm and what happiness is possible. Writes in her notebook: 'Suddenly, life takes us all so seriously.' Watches dawn break over squatted Munich high-rises. Cables slack like arteries. Karla and Renée asleep in their bags somewhere. 'Gazing into this mirror, I realize what has happened.' The area between here and the sea is peppered with military installations. She imagines the species to come: tragic like all conscious life. The train passes insane asylums, electricity plants, warehouses, abandoned docks. Traces of the European War. Handles life like a sacred weapon. No longer young, she has fewer illusions. This place doesn't symbolise anything, she thinks bitterly, except perhaps its own haunting. Freedom is what? To take drugs and eventually commit suicide? To fuck without empathy? At least the fighters had beliefs and values. From the train, glimpses through smashed-out windows at vases, framed pictures, glasses and cups. Everything scorched and blackened – romanticism at its most ruthless. Parable of the human condition: 'The misery of man without God.' (Canned laughter.) What are they looking at? They ruined everything. Demolished the monasteries and churches. AK-47s in every photograph, enchanted by their own manliness. Now we douse our pain with alcohol and chants. Passing old statues like a graveyard, she writes in her notebook: 'All philosophers hitherto have merely changed the world; the point is to destroy it.' Landscapes of our mad desire. Journey on, through this night. The train will never reach its destination.

The lovers are strangers here. Entertaining doubts about their own existence, they see the headlights of a car on the far side of the square. (Just some couple in a hell of their own.) She smiled girlishly, pushed a wisp of hair back from her face. 'Life is to be ruined.'

Morning. Sunlight falls through the guesthouse windows. The repetition of this situation across aeons. A few descendants ... He understands the appeal of cave-painting, even if he has never succumbed to art. After shaving, he finds her quiet and pensive on the bed. 'I've been away a long time,' he says, towelling his chin. 'I know. Years.' 'Longer. We have to consider where all this will lead.' Of infinite richness, this life. At least, that's what she thought then. It's true, she had been unable to resist temptation, hurling herself at all those strangers, but at least her heart was open. She caught him by the arm. 'There is nothing I didn't give you.' Tears of hatred, an inner violence that astonishes her. ('My father's daughter ... Where is she?') The square outside the window is deserted, she notes absently. Life evaporates from morning streets. Soon even our memories will be gone. We'll dissolve in the earth with the worms, but before that day, my body will light up brighter than supernovas, and you will not be the one to know it, though it will burn you. She kneels before him, pulls down his trousers, looks up in his eyes, communicating so much. He gasps. *One of you is close to tears, the other close to death.* She draws her fingertips along his cock, tweaks the tip, how he likes it. Takes him in her mouth, hears him whimper as if in remorse. Noon falls. Shadows drift across the room. (Seen from outside the window, the room is empty.) Later she sleeps, her shorts and knickers round her ankles. The door is ajar. Faint breeze stirs the open curtain, she moans softly, raises a leg to find him (not there). He boards a train and goes back the way they came.

*

'Consciousness: the condition of being locked outside of life. We press our faces to the glass.' (Standing ovation.)

*

Even those with noble motives wake with a hangover. Wars no longer end. 'You cannot face your "human animal".' Got no home, not now in any case. Subject is photographed naked, in humiliating poses. 'The perennial madness.' Man is ingenious in how he holds his world together. Disguised as playboy billionaires, they buy yachts, luxury cars and apartments in the major capitals. Channels open from Pakistan. War becomes a metaphor. 'The only arguments I had with him were about cars and baseball.' Things had become too bitter, he said. A headstone somewhere, flowers falling apart in the rain. 'And you call *us* terrorists? If any struggle requires martyrs, it's this one.' Gentle, she said, like a race from beyond ... Mother was a seller in the bazaar – fruit, dates, coffee ... A sobering demonstration for those who can perceive it (footage of mushroom cloud over the Bikini Atoll). 'The major breakthrough had to do with clarity.' 'Who are you, the Thought Police?' Imagine it growing, multiplying, diversifying ... inevitable rise towards consciousness. There's no point being a pessimist about the internet. 'We envy their weapons, their convictions, their pornography.' Shudders. At dawn, driving towards a mosque in Lahore. A harmless lunatic, they said. Soon they'll know better. Emphasise the history of technology – a conscious evolution. Burning outskirts of the world. Now learn to sit back and watch.

3. *A Promise of Happiness*

> 'For years I had been trying to think up stories, narratives, that would give me the excuse to convey, say, a deserted beach, because that – the beach – was what I really wanted to convey. Finally I thought, "Why not simply give them the deserted beach?"'
>
> – *Killian Turner, from an interview with* ZG *magazine, 1981*

Writing page after page, day upon day, remaking himself in a cabin in the woods. A manifesto, he called it. The usual doleful anarchism: 'Systematic genocide of the native people ... Our forced march through territories of nothingness', and so on. Bombast and idle threats. Shrouded in self-made myth and marijuana fumes, a face like the entrance to caves. This painstaking construction of a 'visionary' work. Nothing like a belated revenge, he thinks. Bearded and fervent, like some mujahedin.

*

The rooms the soldiers combed smelt strongly of shit and petrol, and something else too. Dolls and clothing strewn over a dusty floor ... They had entered the city after a wave of high-level defections. Now he peers through his binoculars at the outlying posts and the dunes along the horizon. Fraying fabric of the regime. 'Everything is conditioned by necessity.' 'So much code eventually becomes theology.' Medals of bone and charred flesh. Desert roads buried under dust and rubble. Villages stand deserted. 'This hostile attitude towards all sensuous cultures ...' 'The White Man's burden, pal.' 'The

White Man? I remember childhood afternoons, the particular quality of the sunlight. Oranges dropping from a tree by the train tracks. So ripe, so heavy with sweetness.' Sighs. 'The absurdity of our dreams.'

That night they watched the first bombs fall.

*

Teenage lovers in a shopping-centre café, eating ice creams. Nicole pouts and rolls her eyes. 'After all, there *is* a war on.' '... It's just our insular labyrinth.' 'Are you saying it isn't real?' 'Not exactly. We don't yet know what kind of age is upon us. But it's perfectly real.' Nicole sighs as another song comes on the café speakers. He *never* gets it.

Then Mickey grins. 'You're still my soda-girl pop queen – they'll never take *that* away from us.'

*

The bus trailed over the plains by night. Everyone had nightmares. At dawn they reached the outskirts. She turned to the man in the seat next to her (handsome and silent, he had been staring out the window for hours). Clutching his wrist: 'Cities this vast *must* breed psychosis. *All* cities do.' 'I know. It's always been that way.' Somehow his words pacify her.

*

An unfinished novel by some frazzled drifter, 'Rob Doyle'. He lives near the port. Drugs come in on those ships, I told him. They roll out of town in those trucks down there. (Watches from the hilltop vantage.) Enough coke, heroin and hash to feed this entire junkie nation. He says: 'I think you've just seen too many films. Films distort reality.' 'It's the other way around.' (Howls of laughter.)

'What was the novel about?' I asked him once over kung-pao chicken. 'A man who lives in the woods. There are cannibals, anarchists, and a priest who can't forgive.'

*

Vienna at twilight, a sumptuous dissolution. 'Everything is in decline, and always has been.' From our hotel, a view over the canals, dazzled with evening light. 'Sure, I'll have to live without tobacco and sex for a time, but men have faced starker destinies.' We read on the balcony till we grew tired. Then I turned to him and said, 'Choose escape and individuation ... follow a lonely path, even if it leads to mountain-solitude where only lakes reflect you.'

Down there, the thieves disappear in the backs of cafés. Existence consents to its own ruin. That night he dreamt of landscapes we have never visited, at least not together – small towns, canyons, immense quarries. There is an inner core to him I'm no longer privy to, despite the telepathy.

'He will never finish that novel,' he says the next morning. He is my partner and I love him.

*

'All works of art are unfinished, anyway.' ... 'Faggot. A genuine talent impresses the women and subjugates the weaker men. Thrash about all you like, I know a drowner when I see one.' 'I write for posterity,' he says, laughing bitterly.

*

In a drab provincial hotel room. Mingled smells of many vaginas. Other men's sweat on this bed. (Thinks of a girl from the past whose vagina had an overpowering smell, vaguely aroused by the memory.) In Naples a whore sucked me off in a room like this, I couldn't manage to come ... But Nietzsche lived in such a way, he thinks, dancing naked in a frugal room in Turin. Every day a ledge between the prison and the madhouse. 'My love, all the world is aflame.' Tenderly: 'Ignore the past.' 'Love of my life!'

Watches films with no sound in scarcely furnished Belgian lodgings, or empty cinemas in undistinguished German cities. 'All this furious activity ... Is it merely a prelude to universal war?' She can't utter the phrase 'spiritual struggle' without a sneer or tragic irony. Postcards to her sister out by the Pacific: 'A sky bereft of sun, yet still blue, still containing birds ... Moorish cafés at noon ... "Beauty is a promise of happiness".' Twilight, late summer, the burning sun ...

Absurdity of our dreams.

*

He emerged from catastrophe clutching a red bandanna. Collaborators. Failure and destruction. That vulgar being, 'God' – son of a war criminal ... Recuperates in Paris for a few months, then slips back across the border to Spain to ignite the Republic. 'No one knows – not even God!' (Hysterical laughter.) A tormented community, but such beautiful women ... 'I would gladly give up my life for one night with her.' The older man laughs. 'You may not need to.' Inland, he enters the Basque Country. 'We crouched around the radio all night when we heard the capital was falling.' 'My child, remember this day.' 'Yes, Papa.' Gunmen with the certainty and zeal of youth roar slogans as they storm through the streets. 'I've seen all this before,' says the old woman. 'Don't ask me to applaud your fervours. Just let me dissolve like the rest of nature.' (She's seen it a million times, literally.) Piety and patriotism, the dignity of any creed at all. A nation is reborn.

I wake in a hotel room with the taste of petrol in my mouth.

Loch Ness

We were hitchhiking on a freeway at the limits of the capital. The situation incited a fearful joy. 'Cruelty? That's just like you.' 'This is my country, I don't have to tolerate anyone.' '*Natürlich*,' I replied. Cars zoomed past us, a monstrous violence inherent in the world today. We were young and in love and nothing else mattered.

*

Watching the dreary procession, standing over her grave in the rain ... I remember the day like a death sentence. 'Nothing will ever be the same again.' Once, during a trip to the provinces, she told me that being alive is just like staying in a hotel. 'Then again, when you're in a hotel, you may as well have sex,' she added huskily.

*

Rob Doyle out walking along the cliffs on a grey afternoon. His lips move, he talks to himself, frowns for no obvious reason, makes sharp gestures with his hands. 'You're a tourist, and you're disappearing just like this coastal land.' He ignores my voice and gazes out to sea. 'I wish I had one day of life to spend in pure happiness. I also wish I had a dog, having proven already that I can't live with women.'

Still this struggle to write, fretful and serious in a house on the coast. Listens through the wall to his neighbour having sex, though he was under the impression that she lived alone. 'Maybe she's not having sex.' One bad review and he almost dies of it. Doesn't leave the house for nearly a week. I email him a quote from Ezra Pound: *Ignore criticism from men who have never written notable works.* To which I add, 'For comfort, bear in mind the unreality of life.'

*

Visits the grave of E.M. Cioran in Montparnasse cemetery with a slender blonde who stands slightly back, her features suggesting keen observational faculties and a cool temperament. A cloudy afternoon, the cemetery all but deserted. 'This is as fine a place to make love as any.' They lie down together and couple efficiently, though without any great passion. 'Beckett is buried here too,' he murmurs afterwards, fixing himself. She remains sitting on the ground for a spell, silently contemplative. 'Pessimism as a philosophy is about as interesting to me as heavyweight boxing.' They go for coffee in a nearby café.

*

Phrases from the philosophers of Despair start appearing on advertising billboards: *Man? A twilight sigh ... All thought craves the Night in which it will capsize ... Gaze into the corpse – know thyself!*

In a nearby motel, the champion fighter holds his head in his hands. 'I've lost my ferocity. May as well be a limp-dick sonofabitch.' His young wife (blonde, Caucasian) tries to soothe him: 'Don't fret, baby.'

'I fear everything.'

Their marriage dissolves.

*

Done with hitchhiking, we perch on a hillside overlooking the freeway, out where the billboards are. Binoculars, a blanket, a selection of cheeses, two wine glasses. 'Cities are becoming conscious, let's hope they're benign.' Through the binoculars, she sees a car with tinted windows glide towards the desert.

'You love me. But is it for ever? Youth is fleeting, a wild fuck astride a grave. In a matter of hours we'll have changed beyond recognition.'

*

She can never tell her husband about the erotic dreams she has of heavyweight boxers. Black, glistening men who make her cry out in her sleep. 'I'm a brutal tyrant, a vicious ruthless killer, I live on fear and nails, there's no one like me.' When she wakes, she still loves him, but her love is frayed at the edges by contempt and a mild disgust. Lying beside her, he smiles and looks towards the ceiling, speaking softly of his hopes, always of his hopes. Men are redundant, she decides, little more than playthings. This year, she will take a holiday alone. Madagascar, Barbados, Jamaica ...

*

Another billboard: *Your bitterest enemy lives in your own home.*

*

'I wasn't looking for the "Grand Love".' He cracks open a beer and slugs savagely. 'You have *no idea* how hard I've worked to keep this family together.' 'Yeah well, all I ever learned from you is the art of skulduggery. Is that what marriage is? That and nothing more?' They agree to stay together for the kids, though they soon fuck them up. (Round of applause.)

Saddest thing I ever heard.

The Closest I Ever Got

A dead body rolled up in a carpet and kicked down the basement stairs. The barman kept pouring till all the glasses over-
flowed. 'It's worth it in the end.' 'Not really,' said the blonde.
'Aggressive, ready for violence – the usual sexual competi-
tion between young men. I get it everywhere I go.' This broad
drinks to forget, the barman thinks.

*

A fountain in the main square. An Australian psychologist
admiring the quality of the European light. Those glamorous
years ... The same canals, the hot, sensual cities. A beautiful
girl on the back of a motorbike, rides off down the Calle de
Noche Triste. Traces of a higher culture, though all of that
has long passed ... A young author types rapidly with the
blinds drawn in a small, hot apartment (green T-shirt, trilby).
Hearing the laughter of teenagers down in the street, he sighs,
then goes out and stands on the balcony. *Black lace panties.*
The phrase captivates him; he returns to his desk and types it
out seven times, then stares at the screen, mesmerised. The
teenagers are flirting. A boy in a black leather jacket rides
off on his Vespa with a girl whose body justifies everything.
Later, the author opens a bottle of port and weeps.

*

Through cigar smoke, they regard the loose pages: shards of
text, impressionistic photographs, a semi-coherent polemic.
'Pessimistic novelists, a veritable production line of them.
What are they trying to do, overthrow our civilization?

They'll only overthrow themselves.' 'One of them has made a million since last February … Anyway, how do you know the blonde has beautiful eyes?' 'Because every time she walks into a bar, some guy buys her a drink.' They say nothing, sip their cognac. Two jaded ex-revolutionaries, sitting in this sepulchral bar all week, like they're afraid. This stale, stinging air.

*

Young people on a beach, preparing a meal. It's an overcast day, a little windy. 'Eat something.' A dog sitting on the bonnet of a car, seems to know more than anyone. The exceptional beauty of these girls. 'I couldn't eat another morsel.' … 'No god lingers in my blood.' A poet masturbates in a cave, out where the rocks are jagged.

When the tide comes in, the youths have disappeared.

*

Madam's erotic dreams … Fearsome tyrants butchered on camera – the embassy in flames – 'We reject in the strongest terms this –' Hot tongues of mongrel dogs. They approach slowly and lick the glass … She wakes drenched in sweat, panting. All this opulence, yet so many nights since she's had a man beside her. Every woman needs it.

*

'Your father's dead,' says her teacher. The gamine Nicole has always had troublesome fantasies. Now they might become real. 'Take me.' They fall together, a pleasure intimating total annihilation. 'All I want is to vanish from the earth,' she whimpers as he moves inside her. 'With you!' The teacher's urgent words: 'We are not bound to "real life", nor to their shitty morality.' He comes inside her with a howl.

The blonde girl kneels down and takes it. Pornography, shot-guns, occasional music. (In her latest painting, crucifixes line both sides of the autostrada to Salerno, a groaning fascist on each one.) At first I made her read the Marquis de Sade aloud while I explored her with my fingers. But Christ – that girl soon brought me to my knees. In a voice as delicate as an hourglass: *Love is best conveyed with the fist.* Against a severe desert sky, a towering phallus glistens like an obelisk. 'Past the age of twenty-four, men just don't fuck the same,' she tells her friend over the phone. 'Sexual morality ... cruci-fixes ... Men are terrified, and they're right to be. I'm young, sexy, and as beautiful as death. Tell me that's not power!'

I wasn't insane. I had sought a return to animal life, that kind of debased magnificence. The next time we met, she dangled the keys in front of me. Then she locked the monotonous hotel room from the inside. 'I've always had a thing for panting blondes.' 'You and everyone else.' She made me slide a finger in her asshole. I could feel flakes of shit against my fingertip. My breath in her hair, on her neck. Nothing had changed. 'You get happier, and more fatalistic.' Brazen and vulgar, as intoxicating as an open sewer. The closest to love I ever got.

4. *Baby, the West Will Fear Us*

Passion festers within the camp perimeter. The odour of dust, excrement and coffee seeps into the affair itself. She looks at him now with mistrust. Writes her nightmares in notebooks she conceals in her mattress. ('In this mirror full of screams.') On the walls of the camp, relief maps, aerial photographs, refugee statistics. All that textual babbling. Midnight in the canteen: 'Your attitude is bizarre and sometimes sickening.' 'Look, just tell me you won't make an issue with my wife.' 'We have nothing more to talk about.' Out here, all tensions are exacerbated. Desert truth.

*

You talk often about nobility, but what do you know about shame? Cacophony, dissolution, this eternal fucking world. Cities teem with men like me and our torturous intrigues ... He began to shudder and then scream. Stagnant, atrophied, patently homosexual, he rides the night train from end to end and back again. The only therapy he can afford. Beneath this city, such feelings, these rabid eyes. Men like me become a threat. Men who brood in small rooms with bad air. Listen. Soon you will see my face on every screen in this nation. He carries photographs of Moscow and St Petersburg in his breast pocket – street signs, buildings, blurred shots of obscure functionaries and minor celebrities. Shakes his head disgustedly – these infirm men and their ideological drivel. Poverty is not a crime! The beast in us wants to be whipped. I will *step up*. The night train hurtles through diseased cities – his bad mind. Tyre factories, power plants, slums that seethe with venereal sickness and every kind of plague. He'll feel better at daybreak, he tells himself. That's if I live that long. There is nothing to do but recall childhood and try to stay calm. Days later he awakes in a rented room in another city. I keep myself alive only out of hate, and habit.

*

Madman painting in his studio. Psychiatric outpatients' home on the edge of a vast park in the middle of the city. Calls these paintings his 'blue series' – a wilful provocation. The medication suppresses his sense that the territories are being overrun (migrants, refugees, terrorists). 'Silence please.' Panic in the air like a rectal stench, a –

*

Cop pulls her over on the interstate. 'Need to see some ID.' She looks at him desperately, still clutching the wheel. 'Transgression, the lust for disorder … Officer, I've spent my whole life courting delirium.' Cop shakes his head sadly. 'Out here that just won't ride. Been driving like a crazy person.' And she was so near to the coast – this unceasing ordeal.

*

'In my defence, I was crazed with lust.' The young man stays in his groundfloor room watching porn and taking caffeine pills. Vines from the back garden cover the window. No job, few friends. Says the internet meets all his human needs, bar nutrition. Flatmate is from Belgium, twenty-five, lesbian. Likewise private and reclusive. He rarely sees her. That's not to say he doesn't fantasise. This is to the east of the city, where rents are cheaper. 'I'm out in the future. Symbols are ambiguous …

Stranded in remote territories ... We have known each other for ever.' He dreams of her on a black sea, dying to capsize.

*

Another slap in the face, another abandonment and humiliation. I too have lived in filthy hovels, I too have crawled like an insect. Raskolnikov of the internet age. 'You raise the gun, you transcend all laws.' I fell in love with porn actresses, suffered indignities in the workplace, voted for the lesser of two evils. I watched my *human heart* grow diseased and die before I was twenty-two. What do these leeches know about shame? I'm ten years older than everyone. Ten years that passed like a day. There is no home for people like me.

*

Paris on a midweek afternoon. I was supposed to be writing about a Bulgarian author whose feverish theories had haunted me since college, but my thoughts were sluggish and grim. When it rained I sat in a café and took out my notebook: 'Perimeters ... Reproaches ... A lifetime spent wandering in foreign cities, utterly depressed ... The world holds its breath for a collision it both fears and craves.' Somewhere a door closes. Footsteps in a corridor. He orders another coffee.

*

I liked her but I knew she was insane. So was everyone else in that guesthouse on a lost coast. Ocean like a churning scum, skies of impenetrable grey, motorbikes that passed in the distance – local amphetamine-thugs with a grudge against my civilization. She would walk by herself on the beach for hours, gazing out at the foam. Those days I sat alone in windswept bars, often the only customer. Sometimes there wasn't even a barman.

'Heard he was only here for the sex, and to drink himself into oblivion.' 'Yep.' On a hill out of town, a group of boys strum a guitar, singing intermittently. Everyone seems to be waiting for a calamity, a shattering. I slept for thirteen hours. When I woke, she was gone. A note on the bedside locker said, 'This is a past life.' A few vague lines about a shaman and some ruins.

If I stay here, I will go mad.

*

Autumn in a mid-sized city that isn't particularly distinguished. He's always tired now, sighing and staring into the TV while she's out at work. Sometimes he murmurs about having kids one day, other times he's silent for entire afternoons. Something has been damaged: a fundamental innocence. The daytime talk show host gestures manically. 'Everywhere the sacrament of LSD is being consumed.' Drives with the radio on but remembers nothing. (Music? Talk? Static?) Sees his own emptiness reflected in billboards. By night, watches burning condoms curl up and disintegrate in a deserted car park. They never make love any more.

*

On the afternoon of her twenty-sixth birthday, the Belgian girl drew a bath and opened her wrists. A drowsy, incoherent goodbye. Her flatmate was in his room with the porno. 'She was always insane.' 'We will never make it home, not now in any case.' 'The condition of being locked outside of life.' 'A willing, attractive woman by your side. Days free of all obligation … Does it matter that our sexuality was incompatible? I loved you, in my way.' Burning condoms in a deserted car park. There is nowhere to go.

Utter derision, in this mirror full of screams.

75

*

Interstates, freeways. Drives all night with the radio on. 'I would want, literally, to kill her.' A cuckolded boyfriend – that perennial experience. When something is broken, it's broken. Hears the voice of the talk show host say softly: 'The saddest thing I ever heard ...'

In an early bar on the dusty edge of a city, saves himself only by getting blind drunk. 'How beautiful you were.' Starts weeping and embarrasses the barman (he is the only customer). The barman has no time for this maudlin scene – he looks away. 'Last night the devil stood outside my door ...' It's all coming out slurred. The barman continues to ignore him.

Finally he collapses face first on a table. Everywhere, whiskey and broken glass.

Barcelona

Alicia moved to Barcelona when she was twenty-nine, having ended an eight year relationship after learning of her partner's long term infidelity.

After a couple of months in the city, she got a job as a waitress in a restaurant on the Calle Trujas, on the fringes of the red-light district. She mostly worked nights, and often prostitutes or their pimps or clients would come in, alone or in small, garrulous groups, to eat burritos and kebabs. The prostitutes' clients were drunk and loud, and sometimes they tried to joke with Alicia about their exploits, as if to reassure themselves through her complicity. Many of these late-night customers were foreign tourists. Sometimes they said the most obscene, misogynistic, lewd things in Alicia's presence, not realizing she spoke English. Other times they just didn't care.

On some nights, Alicia was overcome by bitterness and misanthropy. It seemed to her that the Calle Trujas was a sewer, and that the restaurant where she worked was a rotting piece of wood that floated along the surface, on to which rats would crawl and sniff around for a while before lurching back into the fetid stream. Alicia did not have much money: most of what she made at the restaurant went on rent. She could have lived more cheaply if she shared an apartment, but she was determined to live on her own, which she had never done before. Late at night, when her shifts ended, she would go back to her apartment, several streets away on the Calle de la Madera, and sit with the lights off, looking out at the roof-tops, drinking a beer and eating from a box of noodles or a few slices of pizza. When summer came, she sat on the roof terrace instead.

Before I started getting to know her, Alicia had no significant friends in Barcelona. She could have met some had she wanted to, but it felt natural, even enjoyable, to be alone, walking the streets on her days off work, letting her sadness and anger swirl out into the foreignness of the city. She put aside at least half an hour every day to study Spanish, aided by a book and the accompanying CDs which she had loaded on to her phone. On a few occasions, she went for late-night drinks with her colleagues after they had closed up the restaurant. She danced and laughed with them, and they liked her, but whenever they suggested meeting up again soon, she made tactful excuses. On one of these nights out, when Alicia had been waitressing for a month or so, she went home with a slender Moroccan named Salim who worked in the kitchen. Before they made love, Salim stripped his bed of its covers, rolled them up and laid them in front of the window. Alicia did not know why he did this. In the morning, she awoke to find Salim kissing her neck. She drew him in around her, enfolded by him on the uncovered bed. Afterwards, Salim unsheathed the condom and tied it with the tip of his finger in a manner that struck Alicia as delicate and touching. Salim wanted to take her out for breakfast, but Alicia kissed him on the lips and said she would see him in work on Monday night. After that, she and Salim remained friendly, but they didn't sleep together again.

Alicia found a bar that she loved on the Carrer de Paris, one Metro stop away from her home. Sometimes she would go there to write in the notebook she had bought at the Saturday market, or to read, or just to sip coffee, wine or brandy, and watch the locals float in, have their conversations, drift away again. She developed a passion for Chekhov, reading first all his short stories, then all his plays (or as many as she could find in English translation). She also read Kundera, until it came to seem to Alicia that he was engaged in a conversation which excluded her, as if he were unaware she was even in the room. After that, she read Djuna Barnes, Gogol and Jane Bowles. The bar was called Angelino's and it was never full, never empty, and always played appealing music at just the right volume. Once, a couple walked into the bar holding hands. The woman was older, perhaps in her early forties, and wore a red leather skirt and a red top, not unlike some of the prostitutes Alicia encountered at the restaurant. The man was handsomely dishevelled, a decade or so younger than the woman. They sat at the bar and giggled, grinning at one another even as they ordered their drinks, oblivious to the rest of the bar and the world outside. Alicia had been writing about St Stephen's Green, but now she began writing about the couple in Angelino's, imagining the relationships they had both fled to be with each other, the affair they would live out over the coming months – passionately sexual, yet bound on a course for agony and destruction. She wrote about the woman in red standing on a windswept coast, alone, looking out to sea but expecting nothing.

Another evening, Alicia was again writing in the bar. It was already autumn, the sun sinking on the street outside. She did not have to work till the following night. Absorbed in her writing, she was startled when the empty chair by her table shifted. She looked up and saw that it had been moved by a man, who was asking by gesture if he might sit with her. Momentarily Alicia was annoyed that her writing had been interrupted. But the man's eyes were kind. He sat down with her. He wanted to buy her another coffee but she said she shouldn't drink more caffeine. A few minutes later, she let him buy her a glass of Prosecco. He was a big man, with thick arms, strong shoulders and dark, Mediterranean skin. His balding head was shaved and he had a neat, black beard. He laughed softly as he spoke, and listened attentively when Alicia did, nodding faintly. Halid was his name. Around midnight they took a taxi back to Alicia's apartment. They made love till dawn began to show over the rooftops outside the window. Later they stood on the roof terrace in the light of early morning, a sheet wrapped around the two of them to maintain their modesty before any passing seagulls. Alicia later told me they were like two Greek philosophers, and they both giggled like children.

Alicia and Halid met up usually once a week, always on Alicia's terms. When Halid realized that this was to be an exclusively sexual affair, he amiably accepted the situation. They would meet in bars, have one or two drinks, and then go to either Alicia's or Halid's place. If they slept at Alicia's, she would always gently let Halid know, soon after they woke up, that she wanted him to leave. When they were at his tiny apartment in the Barceloneta district, she always left early. Then she got on with her day, smiling spontaneously as she bought vegetables at the market, or took orders from customers, or sat on the roof terrace and listened to the sounds rising up from the street.

It was while Alicia was seeing Halid that I got to know her. I used to take walks around that quarter of Barcelona at night. It was because of Alicia that I often wandered into the restaurant, drinking coffee as the prostitutes and drunken tourists filed in and out. I liked the look of her. Sometimes I would have a book with me and I suppose she saw me as a sort of kindred spirit. Once we had a staccato conversation about Ortega y Gasset while she was between orders. Alicia said she didn't read much philosophy, nor feel the need to, because things were quite simple after all. One night I came in late and lingered while Alicia and Salim were closing up the restaurant. Then she and I went for a drink in a nearby bar.

We drank martinis and Alicia spoke openly to me about her past, the circumstances that had led to her leaving Ireland. She had been in Barcelona six months now, she said. I told her about my art and photography projects, my time spent living in New York and Tangier, and the residency I'd been granted in Barcelona for the next three years.

'What are you working on now?' she asked.

I told her about my project, which was inspired by Molly Bloom in *Ulysses*, and was divided in two parts. First, I said, I took photographs of my subjects as they slept, and made audio recordings of them. I explained that my sound equipment was highly sensitive, able to pick up even the most furtive and intimate noises the subjects made as they slept, including the gurglings and rumblings of their tummies.

'You're a creepy guy,' she said, laughing, then sipping her martini. She had already eaten the two olives on the plastic stick. 'Are they women and men as well?' she said.

'No. Only women.'

'That's even creepier.'

I shook my head. 'I've always been relaxed around women in that way. It's easy for me to be with them, even to stay in the same bedroom as a woman without there being anything sexual to it. I slept in the same bed as my sister till we were eleven or twelve.'

She nodded. 'And so what's the second part of the project?'

'That's when the subject and I exchange beds. So, she spends a few nights in my place, and I sleep in her bed. I record myself as I sleep. I have cameras poised around the bed to take photos of me at intervals throughout the night. Later, I digitally merge the sounds of myself and the woman, the subject. Then I merge the photos. The faces blend together. So do the bodies. Finally I sequence the sounds with the photos. When people are stripped down to that level of intimacy, there isn't much difference between men and women.'

'Do you see yourself as a woman?' Alicia said.

'You mean in life?'

She laughed. 'No, in the pictures.'

I smiled. 'Something like that. It can, in fact, be a bit creepy. But that's part of the fascination. Once, when I merged the photos, I looked exactly like my sister. It was uncanny. It was like ... I felt like I was seeing her ghost.'

I sensed she was curious enough to be my next subject, but I thought it shrewd to wait a while, let her come around in her own time.

Alicia kept seeing Halid, though still no more than once a week. The sex was exciting, yet she never felt any danger that it would lead to more than that, that they would fall for each other. She became friendlier with a short, dark-haired girl from the restaurant called Monica, who was working there for a while before moving to London, where her boyfriend had gone some months previously. 'I haven't been entirely faithful to him,' Monica told Alicia one night when they were having a beer in the restaurant after closing up.

'Has he been faithful to you?' asked Alicia.

Monica shrugged. 'I don't know. Probably not. I don't want to know. It's something we talked about, that it might happen, and if it did, it's better not to know. Anyway, I think about this question, and you know, I reached the conclusion that there is a higher law than monogamy. A higher law than monogamy and fidelity. Sometimes it seems to me that the sin is not to be unfaithful, but to *not* be unfaithful. I mean, in certain situations.'

'Do you really believe that?' said Alicia.

'I don't know,' said Monica, laughing. 'Sometimes.'

Monica took Alicia out clubbing. They would meet beforehand at Monica's apartment to drink a couple of beers and smoke some grass with her friends, who gamely encouraged Alicia's middling Spanish and fledgling Catalan. One night they took Ecstasy before they headed out to the club. Alicia had only ever tried the drug once, years earlier, but it had been an ugly night that ended in an awful fight with her ex-boyfriend, who had grown jealous. This time, with Monica, the drug carried Alicia on to a plateau of bliss that, at twenty-nine, she was astonished to have never before attained or even suspected was possible. The club was a cavern of white lights, where beautiful bodies twisted to music that sounded richer and deeper than any Alicia had ever heard. She smiled at everyone, radiating goodwill. She forgave her ex all his lies and lack of self-control. She remembered Monica's talk of a higher law and saw how it might be true. Dancing, she closed her eyes and felt herself into her ex-boyfriend's body, into his mind, when he had made love to another woman. She felt very near to him. Monica appeared out of the crowd and put her arms on Alicia's shoulders. Alicia turned to her, grinning, and they kissed one another on the lips. Monica laughed and merged back into the crowd. Later, the two of them were dancing with a tall, slim young man who had his shirt buttoned low and dark hair on his chest, a grey-black trilby on his head. The girls took more Ecstasy and gave one to the guy. Then the three of them were in a taxi, laughing, kissing, pointing out the window. Whenever the man had nothing to say, he laughed and slapped his thigh, and put his arm around either Monica or Alicia's waist. He took a selfie of the three of them in the back of the cab. At Monica's place, she put on some music and they all got into bed together. The curtains were open and blue light from the street illumined their bodies. As they caressed one another, Alicia found she mostly wanted to kiss Monica, but Monica kept kissing the young guy. Alicia either couldn't remember his name or had never learned it in the first place. Grinning, the man asked the girls to kiss one another while he jerked off. Then he licked Alicia out while Monica sucked and kneaded Alicia's breasts. He wanted to take another selfie of the three of them in the bed, but Monica chucked his phone onto a pile of clothes by the window and started to suck him off. At several points the situation became precarious as one of the girls began to laugh; the man then had to coax them into continuing through caresses and whispers. As the night trailed on in a pornographic blur, Alicia found that Monica and the young man were becoming exclusively concerned with one another. The man was now on his knees and licking Monica out while she clasped her tits in her palms, moaning softly. His dick had gone limp but he jerked it off till it hardened again. Alicia was about to get up to leave, but the guy reached out, not raising his face from Monica's cunt, and drew her in. He guided her hand behind him, gesturing for Alicia to penetrate him with her finger. She did, and as he kept licking Monica out, the young man whimpered and growled, still pulling himself off with one hand. Monica came loudly. Then the young man came – Alicia could feel his sphincter throbbing against her knuckle. He folded down onto Monica's belly with a shudder, sliding off Alicia's finger. He and Monica lay coiled together like that, their fingers entwined. A few moments later, quietly rising from the bed to leave the room, Alicia saw that dark brown spots of shit were flecked over a portion of the sheets. They looked like blood.

She sat out on the sitting room balcony with the lights off, thinking about what had happened. Now and then she could hear noises coming through the wall from the bedroom. Across the city, a plane was flying low and she watched till it vanished beneath the skyline. She made herself a cup of camomile tea. Soon it was dawn. Alicia showered and got back into her clothes, which were pungent with chemical sweat. Then she quietly opened the bedroom door and looked at the couple – they were naked and sleeping like infants, hand in hand on the strewn and spotted bedding. Alicia closed the door and left the apartment. She hailed a taxi on the awakening street and went home.

In October, Alicia received an email from her ex-boyfriend – the first time he had contacted her since the separation. He said he was sorry, profoundly sorry; he said he had been looking deeply into himself and at the pain he had caused, not only to her but throughout his life to those who loved him, and was ready to change. He said he wanted her back. He said he fully understood why she had left, and would never hold it against her, but now things would be different. He said he was ready to be a father, if that was what she wanted.

For days after reading the email, Alicia's emotions were in turmoil. Suddenly it seemed so appealing: to get out of Barcelona, this city she had landed in with no purpose other than to be away from Dublin; to go back to the life she'd had before, but altered now, with greater power on her side. Then the weekend came, and she met Halid for a drink. They drank more than usual, laughed easily, and talked more intimately than ever – lacking any sense of consequence, Alicia felt she could be as honest as she liked with Halid. She told him about her ex, his affairs and one-night stands, how she no longer believed there was one person with whom you ought to share your life, but perhaps many, or no one in particular.

'Were you ever unfaithful to your boyfriend?' Halid asked.

Alicia trailed a painted fingernail down the side of her cocktail glass. 'Once,' she said.

'And did he know about it?'

'No. I never told him, even after I found out all he had done on me. Of course I considered telling him out of revenge, but I realized I just didn't want to. It was with one of his best friends, years ago now. It was just one night.'

'And do you regret it?' Halid asked.

'No,' she said. 'Not then, really, and definitely not now.'

They took a taxi to Halid's place. At a certain point in the night, her brow mussed with sweat, Alicia leaned her face in close to Halid's. She said to him, 'There's a thing I've always fantasised about doing, about a man doing to me, but I've always been too embarrassed to tell anyone.'

Halid grinned. 'Tell me,' he said.

The following morning, for the first time, Alicia felt tempted to stay for breakfast, maybe to go for a coffee and read the papers with Halid, then walk with him in the park or to the weekend market. She resisted the temptation. When she got back to her apartment, she deleted the email from her ex: she would stay in Barcelona for another year, maybe longer, maybe a lifetime. In the middle of the following week, she called Halid and explained that they would not be seeing one another again. Halid sounded deflated, but said he understood.

Not long after that, Alicia texted me to say she wanted to be a subject in my 'sleepy project', as she put it. I spent a night at her apartment on the Calle de la Madera. As usual, I brought along a sleeping bag and pillow, to lay out on the floor in case I got tired. However, Alicia insisted that I should lie in the bed with her instead. By five a.m., I had taken almost two hundred photos. Alicia had shifted only once in the course of the night, turning from her side to lie face-up. Careful not to disturb the microphones that were directed at various parts of her body, I gently lifted the covers and lay down beside her. The bed was not large, and I inadvertently brushed her side with my hand. The warmth of her body triggered memories of my sister, from years ago. I imagined what would happen if Alicia were to wake and turn to me, or reach out her hand for mine beneath the covers. I found my heart was beating violently.

Mexico Drift

The last time I saw my friend Julian was the night we went to see Bret Easton Ellis give a talk at the London Literature Festival. Most of what follows I learned from a long, discomfiting email he sent me from Guatemala, out of the blue, more than a year later. I received that email seven months ago; I've heard nothing from him since.

The Bret Easton Ellis talk took place on a drizzly autumn evening two nights after Julian's twenty-ninth birthday, which meant we were both still a little fragile from the effects of all we'd consumed at the riotous party that had doubled as Julian's big send-off (he had quit teaching at the language school where I'd met him and booked a one-way flight to Mexico).

After the talk, over glasses of Leffe in a pub across the river from the South Bank, we discussed why seeing Ellis had been so dispiriting.

'He's the dead fucking end,' Julian said.

His voice was strained. He was drinking quickly to become interested in where he was.

'You know what I mean? Being totally nihilistic is exciting when you're younger, you can get away with it then. There's still pleasure to be had in the destructive work. You haven't yet had to live in the ruins. Most people who're like that seem to wise up and realize it's like this fire they've set in themselves, and if they don't put it out by a certain age, they'll be consumed. All that'll be left are the ashes. That's the impression Ellis gave me: a man of ashes. He showed too keen an interest in the fucking void, and eventually it started taking an interest in him. He should've killed himself twenty years ago.'

I drank my beer as Julian peered into his glass. Memories reeled through my mind: Julian as the younger punk-intellectual, at war with everything, but winning the war and exhilarated by the fight; the acts of vandalism, all the fire-gutted cars and shattered McDonald's windows. And later, the deepening sullenness, the first flirtations with far-right ideologies, the sneering disdain for younger advocates of the same radical leftism he had once espoused.

We got mildly drunk that night, but Julian never shrugged off his lethargy. We said goodbye at Leicester Square tube station and I took a bus home through the rain. Less than a week later, Julian flew to Mexico City, alone.

For his first few days there, he saw no one. He drank and wandered the streets, the city a choking carnival of noise and pollution. He hooked up with some punk contacts; vague friends of vague friends squatting in the city and playing in hardcore bands, angry and self-marginalised. An identical scene exists in hundreds of cities across the world, depressingly homogeneous and homogeneously depressed.

Julian left the squat one morning without saying goodbye.

He took a taxi to the bus station and began travelling around Mexico: Guadalajara, Chihuahua and Ciudad Juárez, where (he wrote) he hoped to witness a drug-war shootout, 'or even be slain as an innocent bystander'. He found a dive bar in Juárez where he watched a gig, getting very drunk and taking speed given to him in the toilets by a young, almost effeminately beautiful punk, no older than nineteen. Julian's Spanish was rudimentary but he befriended the Mexican and somehow explained that he didn't have anywhere to stay that night. 'No hay problema,' said the young guy, 'quédate conmigo.' Julian didn't remember getting home or into bed, but later he was woken by the young Mexican unbuttoning his boxers and taking his cock between his lips. Julian's head spun as he ran his fingers through the guy's curly black hair. He came into his mouth. The boy gently spat out the come on Julian's leg and swirled his finger through it, like he was painting a spiral on his thigh. Then they kissed until Julian passed out.

He left the next morning and took a bus to another town on the edge of the desert, where he hung around for a few days, reading Alberto Moravia in cafés and walking out at the periphery. He had sex again, this time with a barmaid from a place he got drunk in one night. She lived with her sister and Julian could hear her snoring in the next room while they fucked. They didn't use a condom. Later in the night, as Julian lay in the dark with his eyes closed, he heard the woman weeping beside him. He left in the morning. After drifting for another couple of days, he arrived at Caborca, a desert city where more punks he knew were squatting. One of these was Sebastian, a Mexican who Julian had known six or seven years previously, in Madrid. Back then, Sebastian was twenty-five and still ablaze with youthful idealism. Now, that fire had all but burnt out. The world had not changed like Sebastian had demanded it to, but had moved on without him, brash with sunshine and thoughtless laughter. Like so many punks past their mid-twenties, Sebastian had begun to re-channel the aggression of his fading youth into a world-hating defeatism.

The building that Sebastian and his friends were squatting was a crumbling four-storey block on the desert-whipped fringes of town. There was a large courtyard in the middle, hemmed in by the pale walls of the abandoned apartments. In this court-yard the punks would pass their days drinking, smoking weed, sometimes screwing one another, and playing music when they could be bothered to on battered amps, guitars and a rusted drum kit, though their songs were all at least five years old and they seemed to spit out the rebellious, leftist lyrics with bitter irony (all of these punks were in their late twenties or older). The numbers fluctuated but there were usually around eight of them staying there. Mostly they were Latin Americans.

Sebastian's girlfriend, Erika, was an Argentinian who said she'd never go back to that country, so vacuously obsessed was it with image and surface. Julian would watch her through the late-afternoon tequila blur, when the sun's glare dragged all of existence out into the open, groaning, exposed and humil-iated. Erika seemed strangely indifferent to Sebastian, who grew more sullen and withdrawn as the days and weeks piled up, loitering at the far end of the courtyard with his dark curly hair and his Misfits T-shirt. The couple had an open relation-ship, but neither Erika nor Sebastian ever seemed bothered to fuck any of the other punks, perhaps because the permu-tations had already been exhausted. After he'd been there for a couple of weeks, Julian followed Erika into the shade of one of the rarely used rooms, up on the third floor. There was nothing in the room but a bare mattress. They fucked for hours in the hot afternoon as Sebastian and the others drank in the courtyard below. Between bouts of screwing, while he and Erika took hits on a plastic bong, Julian could hear Sebastian's voice, unnaturally loud, sometimes igniting into harsh and mirthless laughter. Then there would be silence for a while, the nullifying presence of the desert drifting over the apartment block like a cloud of sand or slow gas.

'What do you think is up with Sebastian these days?' said Julian as they lay side by side, stoned and separate, gazing at the ceiling while intermittent shrieks rose up from the courtyard.

'Nothing's up with him,' said Erika. 'He's unhappy. Why wouldn't he be?'

Julian snorted. 'What, cause he never managed to change the world? He needs to grow up. I don't have any pity on him.'

'You don't have pity on anyone. And no one has any pity on you.' She laughed.

'That's not true,' said Julian, tiredly. In the courtyard someone played a grindcore band on an ancient cassette deck and Julian began to fuck Erica with his fingers, while she stroked his cock, gently at first but soon tugging violently, so that they came almost together, juices spilt on leather and dust as the slow, turgid warp of grindcore bounded off the walls.

He stayed on in the squatted block. Days rolled past like the occasional, slow clouds in the desert sky, or the lone cars on the highway that trailed silently to the horizon. A guy called Raoul came up from Mexico City with a great deal of speed. For three days they all stayed up getting wrecked. It was fun, like the old days. On the second night of the speed blitz, Julian screwed Erika again. This time it was vicious, both of them snarling, biting and clawing, the border between lust and battery obliterated. 'Spit on me,' she hissed as he held her legs back and plunged into her, wanting to stab and maim and lacerate. His saliva slapped the skin above her eye. She punched him hard in the jaw and he slapped her with equal force so that she let out an involuntary whimper. He felt his cock throbbing hard inside her. At one point Julian turned and saw someone standing in the doorway, the figure indistinct in the gloom. He thought it was Sebastian but couldn't be sure. After a while the figure turned away, indifferent, and Julian gushed into the heat of Erika's pussy, then collapsed on to her chest, wheezing as arrows of light flashed on the screen of his eyelids. He felt alone and serene in the empty drift of time. Nothing had ever mattered and why should it now.

When the speed was gone the group got back to drinking, smoking weed and hanging around. The atmosphere seemed to have deteriorated, even when the after-effects of their drug bender had worn off. Occasionally they ate some half-hearted vegan fare, attempting to quell the sickly heave of their guts. Julian perpetually had the runs, as if something inside him had melted or ruptured. It was like someone was wringing out a filthy towel in his bowels. He didn't screw with Erika any more. Maybe it was time to move on. But Julian was unable to summon the will to break out of the inertia that hung over the block. He didn't really care. The insidious thing about depression is that it snuffs out the desire to do anything about it, negates the notion that there's any compelling reason not to be depressed. He thought he'd been at the squat for five weeks but he couldn't be sure.

One afternoon Julian got back from the town with two bottles of tequila. Five or six of the punks sat in the glare of the courtyard, drinking straight from the bottle. Erika was even quieter than usual, staring as if into an invisible daytime campfire, sighing every now and then. Sebastian too was silent: he had hardly spoken in days. After a while, he took a deep swig on the bottle and walked away, into the gloom of the building. Someone put on a tape, an Arizona sludge-metal band, the awful sound of empty time, the abysmal truth of the desert, of all existence tumbling in the void. As they sat amid the drone, something made Julian look up: on the rooftop, veiled by the sun's glare, stood Sebastian. He was gazing down into the courtyard below. Julian used his hand to block the sun, and watched. None of the others had noticed that he was up there. Sebastian stood very still, never once glancing towards the group far beneath him. Then, without prelude, he let himself fall forward, on his knees. He dropped from the rooftop and plummeted past the fourth, third, second floors. There was a thud and a flash of dust and he fused with the concrete. Julian cursed. The others all turned in the same instant. Sebastian had impacted head first; his top half was flattened into a puddle of swirling human colour. His back half rose out of the fusion in low mounds, like the *mesa* on the empty expanse of the plains.

Erika and the others wouldn't accept that Sebastian had killed himself. When, after a couple of days had passed, Julian tried to persuade them that that's what had happened, they turned on him, hissing that he was scheming and malicious, he thought it was all some fucking game, he should fuck off back to England or anywhere else as long as it was out of their sight. Julian stayed one more night after that. The following morning he gathered his things. On his way out of the squat he took one last look at the patch of concrete where Sebastian had landed, which first the police and then the punks had hosed down. You could still see the blood, a rusty brown smear like a diarrhoea stain. Julian knew it would be there for ever, or at least long after the punks had moved on, or died or grown old, or just walked out into the desert to be felled by the sun. No one was awake to say goodbye when he left.

Anus – Black Sun

I found the video in the small hours, lodged in the murky peripheries of a horrendous porn site, the kind set up by Ukrainian deviants and then abandoned, forgotten, left to fend for itself in the wastelands of cyberspace. A kind of obscene and feral orphan, roaming the void, howling in abjection.

I had come home from a warehouse party and was off my face. I don't know what kind of craving was in me that night. Restlessly I clicked through a series of conventional porno clips, leaving each one behind after a few seconds. Nothing was enough; I wanted something harder. I clicked on links that led to links that led to links – the infinite nexus of the internet, like the fabled Tora Bora caves that Bin Laden was said to have haunted.

The video I eventually uncovered, I have never forgotten. I clicked the flesh-filled thumbnail to begin streaming, noticing with surprise that the clip lasted forty-three minutes.

On the screen, in a window surrounded by ads so vile I felt soiled whenever my vision strayed to them, there was an anus, in close-up. It did not look dissimilar to the anal close-ups common in standard porn clips. Yet this one did not move. It was not a still image, however: there was a constant, subtle shifting of pixilation, and the low hum of background ambience – someone was filming the anus. My jaws gurning, I gazed uncomprehendingly at the gaping aperture nestled between taut buttocks. It was a pert anus, slightly strained, as if the woman (it was clearly feminine) was on all fours. But that was it. No penetration, no other organs, no agent of pleasure or violation. And no narrative – not even of the ultra-minimal variety favoured by modern pornographers, in which all extraneous details of character, plot and setting are effaced, leaving only the pure event of organ-in-organ-in-motion, and the hyperbolic wails of phantasmagorical desire.

An anus, nothing more.

I tried to skip ahead but the video would not allow it. So, I let it play on, and watched, and waited. Nothing happened. Yet, as I watched, I began to feel a change taking place, not in the image onscreen, but in my perception, in myself. It was akin to the onset of a trance. Devoid of all context, even that of the body to which it belonged, the anus began to assume an abstract quality. It became unmoored from its functionality, from its historicity, from all sense of reference. It was neither arousing nor repulsive. I am tempted to suggest an affinity with Kant's 'thing-in-itself'. In rapt free association, I began to see in the anus intimations of a sublime geometry, of astronomy, of black holes, galaxy clusters, the swirl of incipient being-in-the-void which is how I envision the cosmic birth. I saw the sun, the black sun shining on a hazed primordial scene; I saw the solar eye, a god of war and carnage sucking everything into itself and rendering being as non-being, matter as void, darkness as light and light as darkness; I saw the all-seeing eye, the third eye of Shiva, the black core of the earth, the infinite sphere of Pascal's nightmares, the silent portal wherein each man, in terror, must confront himself. The abyss from which all things arise and to which all things must return.

Twenty-eight minutes had passed. I realized this with some surprise – my subjective sense of time had fallen away. The screen: still no change, no development. Only the serene and gaping anus, and the soothing lull of ambient sound, like closing one's eyes in an airport. I was awed, and somehow fearful. Scanning myself for the cause of my unease, I realized I was apprehensive that something sudden and monstrous would happen to the anus. I thought of Andy Warhol's film *Empire*, in which we see nothing but the Empire State Building, from a static viewpoint, in real time over the course of many, many hours: there is a celebrated moment in that film when, suddenly, after an immense period of monotony, all the lights in the building are turned on at once – a sublime and whimsical moment, indeed a moment of madness, and the severe freedom of madness. What if some surprise lay ahead in *this* bizarre, unearthly, and, it had to be said, beautiful video that I was watching? Perhaps the film-maker – the man behind the camera – was a sadist, luring me into a trance of vulnerability before unleashing a sight so horrific, I would be traumatised for ever, left pallid and mumbling, fearful of all sex, all anuses.

I commanded myself to become calm. I would watch the video to the end, come what may. Having resolved thus, I began to relax. And nothing happened – there was no *Empire* moment. Just an anus on screen, in real time, close-up. Once more I began to recognize the strange beauty of the film, though

I could not re-attain the state of transcendent resonance I had experienced before my anxieties took hold.

After forty-three minutes, the video ended, as abruptly and inexplicably as it had begun. I shut down my laptop and went to bed, no longer in thrall to fevers of drug-inflamed lust. I have since tried to find the video again, but even the degrading website where I saw it eludes me. I suspect it has been deleted; or rather, that it is still there, but invisible now, floating in the cybernetic mists, a kind of ghost ship.

On Nietzsche

Some time ago, as my twenties drew to a close, I became filled with an overwhelming desire to write a book about Friedrich Nietzsche, whose work had fascinated me since I'd first read him at age nineteen, exhilarated by the grandeur, strangeness and brilliance of his thought. I can see now that the desire to write a book about Nietzsche disguised a deeper, more personal need: to confront and drive out the sense of total futility that had pervaded my life and thoughts for more than a decade, and had driven me to a despair so chronic and total it was no longer even perceptible. By way of a protracted and intensive engagement with the work of Nietzsche I hoped to determine, once and for all, whether there was hope of ever forging a deeper, more sustaining sense of purpose in a world which, it seemed to me, had lost its vital illusions, its grand hopes and its narrative direction.

Most people who decide to write a book about Nietzsche

or any philosopher will probably do so through the university system. And this is what my remaining academic acquaintances urged me to do, one former professor back in Dublin even offering to oversee my doctoral thesis. However, my desire to write about Nietzsche arose alongside another, equally strong desire: to travel, to move, to be elsewhere. I decided I would leave London at the soonest possible moment, in the company of my girlfriend Natasha; I would cram my backpack with books by and about Nietzsche, and work while on the move. Eventually I would stop in some attractive city or town – possibly Turin, where Nietzsche spent his last productive years before collapsing into insanity – and begin refining the notes I'd have made into the first draft of a book.

It was not, however, possible for Natasha and me to leave London immediately. It would take us, Natasha calculated, another four months to save enough money to travel for a year or so, leaving behind the Hampstead flat in which we had both come to feel so trapped. Four months was plenty of time, she said, for me to 'lay the foundations' of my book about Nietzsche.

In the meantime, I turned thirty. This was an interesting event. At thirty, for the first time in my life, I began to dwell compulsively on the reality of my own death. This came as a surprise, not to say a shock. I had believed throughout my teens and twenties that I was the kind of person who thought of death a great deal; in fact I had prided myself on it. But I hadn't *really* been thinking of death, I saw now; I'd merely been hypothesising, or play-acting. The surprise in genuinely confronting my own mortality was that it had less to do with the future – the coffin I'm bound for – than with the past. Specifically, death was knowing that my twenties – those horny, traumatic years – were gone for ever.

As a consequence of turning thirty and feeling the shadow of my own death fall on me for the first time, I looked in the mirror and said firmly that there was no more time to waste, death had my scent now and I needed to be absolutely ruthless and focused on what I wanted to achieve, which was to write a book about Nietzsche. This newfound sense of urgency at first seemed like a valuable asset and a consolation for the loss of my youth. Before long, however, I realized that it had the effect of *inhibiting* me from doing what I wanted, from doing anything at all. The sense of urgency was so strong it became indistinguishable from the most crippling anxiety. I was unable to get down to anything other than worry about the hurtling of time and the blooming fortunes of my peers, most of whom had not squandered their twenties in a fog of drink, drugs, obsessive reading and pointless travel, as I had.

Seized by anxiety, I lost the ability to concentrate, or what little I'd had of it to begin with. I was like an empty can, blown all over the place. Though I had spent my life doing little apart from reading – doing little *so that I could read* – it struck me as a wild presumption and madness to begin writing a book on Nietzsche without having read in their entirety certain other nineteenth century authors who, although having no direct bearing on Nietzsche, nonetheless constituted the deep background for any serious intellectual endeavour involving a subject from that era. I thought about all the significant nineteenth century books I still hadn't read – books which were invariably long and demanding – and the sheer scale of the task inhibited me from reading even one of them. Weeks passed and I read nothing. I just watched YouTube videos or loitered on Twitter, where I saw writers five years younger than me announce the publication of their new books. A few times, unable to bear the internet any longer, I shut down my laptop, took a breath, and actually launched myself into some or other dusty volume. 'This is it,' I would tell myself. 'The anxiety is clearing. A new phase commences, the crisis has passed.' By the time I'd reached page five, though, I'd have the niggling sense that I was reading the *wrong* nineteenth century author, wasting my time on a dispensable book during a period of great urgency. I shouldn't be reading Fichte (say) but von Hartmann, not Weber but Spencer. By page ten or fifteen, this niggling sense would rise to an intolerable howling in my skull. Fighting off panic, I would put away Fichte and switch to von Hartmann – only to quickly feel that I should really be reading Stendhal, or Comte, or whoever. By the end of the day I'd be back on Twitter, all literature abandoned, or else I'd call Raoul, my alcoholic friend, to come out and get hammered with me. (I thought of Raoul as my alcoholic friend as a way of denying my own undeniable alcoholism. What's worse, this is not a revelation that came later on: I knew I was doing it even then, and persisted in doing it.) My mounting anxiety brought with it a heightened need to drink, because only when I was drinking was I able to forget the hurtling weeks, the pile-up of years, and the fact that I wasn't achieving anything at all. And the less I achieved, the more I drank, and the more I drank the less I was able to achieve, until my life consisted of waking up late, going on Twitter, opening a bottle of wine, and finally calling Raoul, my alcoholic friend – who eventually stopped taking my calls.

I found it easy to give up drinking. I simply replaced one addiction, to alcohol, with another, to caffeine. At the time, I didn't realize I was performing such a substitution. I would simply tell myself, over and over, that I had stopped drinking, and then knock back my eleventh espresso of the afternoon. Eventually, it did dawn on me that I was addicted – not to caffeine, or even to alcohol; I was addicted to *addiction*. Without an addiction, my life was arid and pointless. Having an addiction was like having a pet: it was something to worry over and care for, whose essential function was to shield me from the glare of my disengagement and boredom.

During this period, while I was lost in a miasma of caffeine, Natasha needed suddenly to return to Russia because her mother had fallen ill. Though I had never met Natasha's family, I knew they regarded me as a half-mad and wholly malign influence on their beautiful and intelligent daughter, who surely deserved better, deserved the hand of an oligarch or a media sorcerer, not the squalid Hampstead flat of an alcoholic, bookish weirdo. Despite Russia's luminous literary past, the modern Russian hates and abhors books. There is only one thing that the modern Russian hates and abhors more than he hates and abhors books, and that is the people who read them. Russia's luminous literary past, as far as the modern Russian is concerned, *belongs* in the past.

For several days before and after Natasha left for Russia, I was beset by fears that she would not return to London, or else that she would be unfaithful to me during her time away. Natasha had never done anything to warrant this latter suspicion: my insecurities, in truth, stemmed from an infidelity of my own, committed during the vaguely defined beginning of our relationship, when the parameters had not yet been clearly established, or so I had told myself. Even now, four years on, I worried about the slow, secret evolution of this betrayal in Natasha's innermost heart and thoughts, despite her claim to have forgiven me, and the consequences it might yet hatch, specifically revenge or abandonment.

When Natasha left I looked around our flat, trying to tell myself that she would surely return to London because so many of her possessions were still here. These included her cherished red shoes, the ones her father had bought her as a gift when they had spent Christmas on the French Riviera two years previously, and which she had grown attached to in a manner I privately considered darkly Freudian. Those shoes were a guarantee that Natasha would indeed return.

Now, though, with Natasha away in Moscow and a great deal of time on my hands, I could do little but sit in the living room of our Hampstead flat up on the fifth floor, gazing at the wall or the window, immobilised by dread at the scale of the task I had set for myself, and my feelings of utter inadequacy before it. Not only did the authors on my list of background reading remain unread, but every day the list expanded as I thought of more and more authors who, if I were not to read them, would be unforgivable omissions from anything that called itself a *serious* book about Nietzsche. Soon, it began to seem as if, in order to write as much as a single credible page about Nietzsche, I would have to read (or reread) the *whole* of the nineteenth century – and much of the eighteenth, twentieth and even seventeenth centuries as well.

One midweek afternoon I took myself out to Hampstead Heath for a long walk that I hoped would revive my spirits and infuse me with the vitality of the approaching summer. And, out on the Heath, I did feel better – for about seven minutes. Then, without discernible reason, gloom and anxiety overcame me yet again. Roaming on the Heath like King Lear, I felt like blowing my own head off, or fleeing to Bangkok or Vientiane, where I would book myself into a cheap room and slowly drink myself to death, pausing only to fuck whores and write bitter, sarcastic letters to the great public figures of our age, blaming them for everything. Attempting to shake off these oppressive feelings and shady thoughts, I walked for hours on the Heath, pacing from one end to the other, again and again across its vast and undulating surface, by varying and convoluted routes. Had my pacing been witnessed from the air and then graphed on to a map, it seems to me now, the result would have resembled the last work of a depraved Viennese painter before he shot himself in the face.

I thought hard on the course of that long, not to say interminable walk. I decided it was foolish to put myself under the impossible obligation of reading the *entire nineteenth century* before writing about Nietzsche – better to launch headlong into the writing itself, hurl myself at the project with a warlike and fearless mentality. (The image in my mind, for better or worse, was of kamikaze pilots slamming into an iceberg.) In the grip of these thoughts, while traversing the Heath for perhaps the eighth or ninth time as the sunny afternoon gave way to an overcast and chilly evening, I found myself reflecting on my first encounter with Nietzsche, more than a decade earlier. I had discovered Nietzsche's work in a cubicle in the men's toilets in the Dublin Mail Centre, a colossal, grey building in a business park in Clondalkin, where I worked for three awful years starting when I was nineteen, a period when I was dangerously depressed, impervious to all but the most experimental of medications. I hated the place, hated the people, hated myself for being there. The DMC felt to me like a concentration camp or a prison colony out of dystopian science fiction. The incessant noise of the mail-sorting machines made conversation impossible, which was just as well, considering that the workers who'd manned the machines for years and decades were such mindless, half-demented cretins. Bitter and resentful of everything, I calculated that, for at least an hour during each of my four-hour shifts, I could remove myself unnoticed from the workstations and hide in the toilets, where I was able to read. Reading, I felt, would partly justify my having to be in that horrible building, giving my time to those wretched machines and their wretched human overseers. With the machines screaming outside the toilet doors, I settled in and began reading Nietzsche, getting through *The Antichrist*, *Human, All Too Human*, *Twilight of the Idols*, *On the Genealogy of Morals*, and half of *Thus Spoke Zarathustra* over a period of several months. I should have quit the place, but the psychoanalyst I was seeing advised against making any major changes in my outward life, especially ones which would feed into what he saw as my dominant, dangerous tendency: withdrawing from human society into solitude, into silence, into stinking toilet cubicles.

As I paced across the Heath, I grew more certain that the only hope I had of writing something honest, vital and true about Nietzsche lay in attacking the project in a more personal, urgent, even autobiographical manner – to *write in blood*, in Nietzsche's own words. Perhaps, I thought, I should even write about that vile and stinking toilet in the Dublin Mail Centre, in order to discover what *that* said about Nietzsche, or about the post-Christian epoch more generally, if it said anything at all. It might even be possible, I thought, growing increasingly excited by the idea as I tramped over the Heath, to frame my study of Nietzsche around the image of that stinking toilet, which would speak eloquently to any discerning reader of the death of God, the putrefying carcass of God, not to mention the cauldron of depravity and hate underlying Christian slave morality. The filthy toilet *was Christian morality itself*, it seemed to me then, tramping across the Heath. I returned to the flat late that evening greatly relieved, with the sense I had finally discovered a way in to my project. I resolved that, as soon as I left London and began my travels in Europe, I would begin *writing in blood*. I slept soundly that night for what felt like the first time in months.

A few days after that interminable walk on the Heath, Natasha called to tell me that her mother had died. The illness had developed more rapidly than anyone had anticipated, finally proving fatal. Needless to say, Natasha would now be staying in Russia for considerably longer than she had intended. Towards the end of our conversation, she told me in a low, tired voice that it might make sense if I were to begin my 'Nietzsche journey' alone, and she would join me later on, perhaps in Turin.

At this point, just when it was most crucial for me to save money so that I could get away from the wretched Hampstead flat which had begun to feel like a tomb, or like the inside of my own skull, the philosophy tutoring work I had been relying on inexplicably dried up. Alarmed, I emailed the tutoring agency, but my queries went unanswered. I called the office but everyone I spoke to was vague and evasive, suggesting that responsibility lay elsewhere. The suspicion grew in me that this sudden, drastic diminishment in my employment (admittedly precarious at the best of times) was related to a regrettable and worthless story of mine which had been published a couple of years previously in a scarcely credible online 'literary journal'. The story concerned a drug dealer who spent his days hovering on the fringes of parks and children's playgrounds, often masturbating furtively in the bushes, or just squeezing his balls through his trouser pocket. By night he wrote hate-fuelled tracts about 'redneck hordes', 'girly-girls' and 'demon queers', which he posted to Bashar al-Assad, Gerry Adams and Kanye West, neither expecting nor receiving any response. In what I had considered a daring postmodern flourish, I named this hateful and charmless character after myself, though he had nothing in common with me beyond his addiction to salt and vinegar Pringles and an uncontrollable twitch in his left eye. The story, 'Permanent Erection', had been written and submitted in a single evening while I was hammered on red wine, and had afforded Raoul and me a night of fantastic cackling. However, as soon as I had sobered up I realized that publishing this story online, and framing it in such a way that the reader might assume it expressed my own true, shameful fantasies, or else was straightforwardly autobiographical, might not have been the wisest of moves. In a series of increasingly frantic emails to the journal's editor, I attempted to retract the story and have it taken off the internet. None of these emails was even acknowledged. It dawned on me that the online journal had been abandoned after its first issue, and no one was going to bother taking the site down.

Now that my sole source of income had gone dry, and with Natasha on unpaid leave in Russia, giving no indication as to when she might return ('we are a close family,' she muttered frostily over the phone, implicitly criticising my own indifference to family), I realized that it would not be possible to leave London as early as I had hoped. After another long walk on the Heath, I decided there was nothing for it but to *hurl myself* into my Nietzsche project there and then, in our dingy flat in Hampstead, rather than wait till I got to Turin. *Hurl myself into it*, I repeated, standing before the mirror or lying in bed in the morning. *Hurl myself into it*. At first it was a kind of mantra, a declaration of intent and seriousness. Eventually, though, it was just a phrase I repeated to myself whilst doing absolutely nothing. The phrase even began to repeat itself, it seemed to me, of its own accord. This is difficult to explain, and no doubt it indicates nothing so much as my increasingly frayed nervous state during that strange, isolated period, as the summer set in outside my dim, dusty flat up on the fifth floor. But it really did seem to me that the phrase *hurl myself into it* had taken on a sinister life of its own. Sitting in the flat, immobilised by dread, I would hear the words *hurl myself into it* bounding through the dusty rooms and cramped hallway, alien and meaningless. And, whenever I needed to leave the flat to buy more coffee and instant noodles, it seemed to me that the phrase would continue to resound up there, repeating itself tirelessly and insanely, regardless of there being no one present to hear it.

After Natasha had been gone for two months, my fears and insecurities gained such a hold on me that I took to going to bed at night with her red shoes clutched tightly to my chest, under the covers. In truth, I would even have worn them on my hands, or perhaps on my feet, were it not that both my hands and feet were too large for those dainty red shoes, Natasha's devotion to which I fully understood.

It was now the middle of summer. Having no job to go to, and with most of my friends out of town, I rarely left the flat at all. The sense of claustrophobia in the flat was surpassed by my fear of the world outside, which had never seemed more hostile and sinister. Crime in London no longer has any *motive*, I told myself, peering at the skyline through my binoculars. Hooded youths will emerge from the shadows and plunge a knife into your groin, or shatter your bones with iron bars, or beat you to a coma in a park at night, raping your every orifice, all for no reason whatsoever. This new breed of London thug *takes pride* in its absence of motive, I reflected; motive is *shame* to the contemporary London thug, a creature whose thirst for cruelty is without limit. I imagined that the filth and horror of London was a rising tide, and that soon it would rise right up to our fifth floor flat and pour in through the windows, a black tide of filth and horror, drowning everything.

Oddly, such morbid and gloomy thoughts as these, while inhibiting me from leaving the flat unless strictly necessary, also had the effect of liberating me from the dread that had prevented me from doing any work at all. Start with *one true thing*, I told myself in sudden clarity, and the rest would follow. And so it was that, on a bright Tuesday afternoon, with the sound of children's laughter reaching me from the courtyard, I wrote the following sentence:

Chief among Nietzsche's virtues is that he is never boring.

On the one hand, I reflected, looking over the sentence I had just written, this was a stunningly banal point to make. On the other hand, it expressed an important truth. The fact is, I told myself, many of even the very best writers are frequently boring, and not only the philosophers. Take, more or less at random, Don DeLillo, a novelist who I revere: all too often he bores me, I reflected. I sit through his books, enjoying them immensely and yet bored out of my head, tempted at every turn to put the book down and do something less boring, like look through my binoculars at the London skyline. Reading, in fact, is a fundamentally boring activity – which is not to say it isn't the most satisfying thing you can do with your time. In truth, all I did was read, and it's all I've ever done. It was simply that, with so many writers, you have to trawl through the dull parts – sentences, pages, whole dull chapters – to get the hit you're after, the flash of gold in the tilted pan. Ideally, a book would offer an experience of consistent, unrelieved fascination, charged and compulsive in every sentence. Nietzsche, far too impatient himself to permit a moment's boredom, offers precisely this ideal, book after book of it, I reflected.

Reading him is an unadulterated hit, with nothing mediating between the reader and the ecstasy of pure idea. Nietzsche's aphoristic style is itself a strategy against boredom. He knew that reading was boring, and that bad books constituted a grave offence, so he was insistent on not adding to the deluge of books that should never have been written, let alone read. Towards the end, I recalled, he had given up reading almost completely, preferring to walk in the hills and mountains around Turin, by the lakes, given over to the ravishment of his senses and the dance of his mind. Having reflected thus for several minutes, I wrote another sentence:

Reading Nietzsche is like smoking crack –
an unadulterated hit.

After writing this second sentence I felt good enough to take a walk on the Heath. While ascending Parliament Hill, a forest of cranes stretched across the far horizon, it began to seem to me that, in writing about Nietzsche, I was really writing about boredom, confronting the problem of boredom. All activities are boring, I thought then, because being conscious is boring, and although reading is boring too, it is less boring than all other activities. Consciousness, that was the real problem. To be conscious is to be bored, to seek distraction, and reading is among the least boring, most distracting of all boring activities. That is why I do it, and why I don't bother doing anything else, if I can help it, I told myself.

I returned to the flat and, too exhausted to work any more that day, stared at the window till the sun had gone down and it was necessary to stand up and turn on the lamp. Glancing in the mirror before going to bed, I was surprised to find that, without having noticed, I had fallen into a state of what can only be described as severe neglect. Not only did I look dishevelled, as was to be expected, but I looked *like an old man*. And not only that – I also looked *demented*. I looked like a demented old man, a demented old tramp of a man, the kind of person who should not be let near children nor vested with any responsibility whatsoever. My hair, which had been slowly going grey since my mid-twenties (the result, I was told, of a vitamin deficiency I had never bothered to learn about or rectify), had massively accelerated its process of greying, so that overnight, it seemed, I no longer had a head of black hair streaked with grey, but a head of grey hair flecked with little veins of black, tiny pockets of resistance mopped up by a merciless occupying force. The skin beneath my eyeballs sagged like that of a man twice my age. On the whole, I resembled nothing so much as a wilting plant, left in a pot by a window not facing the sun.

The following morning, after a good sleep, and heartened that I had finally made a start on my study of Nietzsche, even if I had written only two sentences, I arose early and went to buy the makings of a decent breakfast. It was a warm day, and I made a point of lingering for a moment at the grocer's counter, issuing what I intended to be a casual remark about the weather. Having eaten breakfast, I shaved carefully, and combed my hair in such a way that the grey did not seem so overwhelming as it had the night before. I made myself a strong, very sugary coffee. In the living room I opened the window to let in some air, and sat down at my desk with sunlight streaming all around, to email Natasha. I told her I hoped she was doing well, and that her family was holding together in *this very difficult time*. I gently suggested she might call or email me soon, the fact being that I hadn't heard from her in quite a while, though of course that was because she was stricken with grief and not thinking about phone calls or emails to a distant boyfriend. I made a jocular reference to her red shoes. Then I moved on to telling her about the development of my thoughts regarding my study of Nietzsche, hinting at significant progress already made. I explained my recent intuition that the core of my project was no longer Nietzsche himself, but boredom, the *existential problem of boredom*, as I put it. Nietzsche was merely the platform from which I could launch this enquiry, this meditation on boredom. Then again, I wrote, sipping my coffee, it was entirely possible that Nietzsche was the *backbone* of a more ambitious and expansive work that would meditate not only on boredom, but on the myriad existential quandaries brought to light by the experience of reading Nietzsche, of which boredom was only one. *If this is the case, I must never stray from Nietzsche*, I typed with sudden vehemence. *Nietzsche is the prism through which I will analyse the human situation in all its multifarious components. I must never stray from Nietzsche.*

I pressed 'send', then got up to make another coffee.

Days passed and I waited for Natasha to reply to my email, or to phone me, but she did neither. I tried calling her Russian number but there was no answer. Days drew out into weeks, time unmarked, indistinguishable time. I spent many hours sitting in the chair, more or less at peace now, contemplating Nietzsche and the study I would one day write of him. The work itself had stalled; I no longer wrote, only reflected, and reread the opening pages of *Thus Spoke Zarathustra*, which I considered the essential Nietzschean passage. I myself was 'the last man'; I understood that now. Mostly I read nothing, sitting in my chair in silence, whole days passing. My fears had dispersed. I would write my book on Nietzsche eventually, and even if I didn't, somehow that was OK too, because I was *living* the book, encountering Nietzsche in a manner which went beyond literature. I knew I would never make it to Turin. I thought often of the filthy and stinking toilet in the Dublin Mail Centre where I had first read Nietzsche; I wondered if it was still in use, whether some earnest, anguished young man was sitting in there at that very moment, discovering the awe and terror of Nietzsche, of a world which was drifting away from all suns, falling as through an infinite nothing.

Summer ended. I had stopped washing the dishes. It was over a month and a half since Natasha's last email, and two months since her last phone call. My savings had dwindled and soon I would have to apply for benefits. I no longer read anything at all. One afternoon I opened my laptop and reactivated my Facebook account for the first time in years. I clicked on Natasha's profile. There, I found a photograph, posted two weeks earlier by someone named Dmitri. The photo was of Natasha, her father and brothers, and several people I did not know, standing in a ballroom at some semi-formal occasion. Everyone in the picture was smiling. Natasha, with an enchanted expression, gazed past the others at this Dmitri, who smiled back at her with a calm, self-assured gaze. Natasha had one hand on her father's chest, and she was wearing a pair of bright red shoes – brighter and redder than the shoes I had been sleeping with for the past several months. After staring at the photo for some time, I deleted my Facebook account and shut the laptop.

In the bedroom, it seemed to me that Natasha's old shoes were no longer as shiny as they had once been, and no longer as red. In fact, it seemed that they were not red at all, and perhaps never had been, but magenta, or wine. I now even recalled, or seemed to recall, hearing Natasha referring to them, not once but several times, as her 'wine-coloured shoes'.

Three Writers

The Glasgow Novels of Malcolm Donnelly

Growing up in a harsh, working-class area of Glasgow, Malcolm Donnelly turned to reading as a means of escape. From his teens onwards, writing served the same purpose. When he was sober, Malcolm's widowed father, Angus, felt inadequate to the task of single-handedly raising three boys while working long shifts at the Tennent's brewery. When drunk, he was no less inadequate, but alcohol dulled his frustration.

In his early fiction, Donnelly took flight from these dismal surroundings, preferring exotic settings and fantastical plots. His first three novels were set entirely in countries and regions where Donnelly had never been: Borneo, Panama, the Maghreb. Rather than alcoholics and Glasgow hard men, the novels are populated by shamanic tribes, arms dealers, pirates of the Malacca Strait, warlords and savages. In short, these were the kind of books based not on personal experience, but on other books – and on movies, comics and cartoons.

It was not until *Blades or Shadows* (1979) that Donnelly adopted his native Glasgow as a fictional setting. The city he depicts is a vision of hell. The dark, polluted streets and piss-sodden alleys bear witness to lives of unremitting bleakness. The pubs where much of the novel's action takes place (though 'action' is a dubious word) are sordid to the point of hallucination. Drinking is constant, joyless and brutal. Sex, when it happens, is cursory and humiliating. Fat, toothless whores grope the cocks and balls of the men who sit drinking lager amid clouds of cigarette smoke. The men listlessly swat the whores away, having scant interest in sex and probably no capacity for it either. A brawny, sullen man who habitually downs three whiskeys for every pint of Foster's he drinks, swings a punch at a particularly foul whore who attempts to entice him by juggling her enormous tits in his face. The punch knocks her to the floor; the other drinkers watch indifferently before returning to their conversations or their pints.

The novel's climax is a long, desultory, expletive-ridden dialogue between Sam, a red-headed youth of twenty-two without prospects, interests or aspirations (he is the novel's protagonist), and a much older man with a drink-ruddy face and a rasping cough, named Phil the Club. The dialogue's binding theme is human isolation: both agree it cannot be escaped (Sam adds: why would you want to?). A huge woman named Jolene, 'with layers of chin you could sink a fist in', briefly joins the conversation. Sam tells her to fuck off. Phil and Sam broach such topics as Scottish independence, page 3 girls, English women, the IRA, Celtic and Rangers, the Queen, the greatest footballers of all time, the greatest footballers of the decade, and infidelity.

At the end of the dialogue, Sam staggers out of the pub to throw up against the wall. Phil the Club (who has drunk as much as Sam, if not more) orders another pint, which he drinks as he has drunk all the others: in three vast gulps. The novel ends with Phil sitting on his stool, gazing into the gloom of the pub. The author compares him to the Buddha.

In *Mitchelmore* (1985), Glasgow is again the setting. The city is evoked no less pessimistically. This time, a series of horrific murders in Glasgow's most run-down areas provides the skeleton of plot on which the novel is fleshed out. Jake Mitchelmore is the detective charged with investigating the murders. Initially he pursues his duty with a marked lack of energy or conviction. It is unclear whether he believes the murderer cannot be caught, or if he simply has no desire to do so. Mitchelmore is a lugubrious man, given to ruminating dourly while gazing into the black waters of the Clyde, or at the faces of the Glaswegians who flow past him on the streets, 'a river of derelict souls, lurching towards Nightmare'.

All of the victims – seven, at the point when Mitchelmore takes on the investigation – are male, between the ages of twenty and fifty-two, and all are football fans. Four are fans of Celtic, two are fans of Rangers, and the other – this is the detail that eventually brings Mitchelmore to the brink of madness – follows Hearts. The men have come to grief on deserted streets or in lanes while returning from the brutal drinking sessions which are the leitmotif of Donnelly's Glasgow fiction. More often than not, the victims are killed by a single blow to the back of the head, sometimes while pissing against a wall.

Two theories are proposed. First, that two killers are responsible, and Glasgow is playing host to a tit-for-tat series of attacks among football fans gone to the dark side. In this theory, one of the killers is a Celtic fan, while the other follows Rangers. (So why did the Hearts fan have to die? wonders Mitchelmore.) Second, that the murders have been committed by a lone individual – a serial killer, though Donnelly refrains from using the term throughout the novel, for reasons best known to himself.

Mitchelmore soon discounts the first theory – the multiplication of motives is dangerous and inelegant. Despite the opposition of his superiors (and his rivals), Mitchelmore knows in his heart of hearts that the crimes are those of a single, profoundly disturbed individual, probably an alienated young man from the inner city whose parents were alcoholics or abusers – a young man, in fact, not unlike Mitchelmore in his youth, before he found his direction in life through a career in the force and a passion for training pigeons.

'I see you,' whispers Mitchelmore one night, drunk, peering out the window of the high-rise flat where he has lived since his divorce eight years ago. 'I know you, I feel you. I ... taste you.'

To the concern of his senior officers, and of Nancy, the social worker with whom he has become romantically involved, Mitchelmore loses interest in anything outside of the football-fan murders. His relationship with Nancy falls apart – Mitchelmore hardly seems to notice. He no longer drinks in his local. He takes to sleeping at his desk, waking with a start to find himself peering at an assemblage of photographs: the victims' wounds; the locations of their deaths; the crowds outside the Ibrox and Parkhead on match days; derelict flats and dank, gloomy hallways with no obvious link to the case. Mitchelmore starts drinking in the inner city pubs once frequented by the victims, concealing his loyalty when in Rangers pubs (he is a Celtic supporter), saying little, watching, waiting (but waiting for what? Even he seems not to know).

His sergeant, Duncan Shearer, suspends Mitchelmore.

'You're losing it, Jake,' he rasps. 'Get a grip, before there's no way back.' Needless to say, Mitchelmore pays little heed and continues his obsessive investigation. One more murder is committed which may or may not be connected to the others: a Rangers fan is stabbed outside a chipper near the Ibrox. Mitchelmore is certain that this is the next killing in the series. By now, the reader has ample reason to doubt Mitchelmore's judgement, indeed his participation in a shared reality. Winter sets in. Mitchelmore, no longer in contact with friends, family or former colleagues, drinks more heavily. He gets into fights. A whore wanks him off down a lane but he is too drunk to come. He throws up. He collapses. Owed rent, his landlord appears at Mitchelmore's flat and finds he has not been sleeping there with any regularity. The muted roar of inner city Glasgow closes in over Mitchelmore. Christmas arrives. The city is cold, and silent but for the wind blowing through the lanes, past shuttered-up pubs and factories. A child cries in the distance. A dog whimpers and gnaws on its own leg. Here the novel ends.

After *Mitchelmore*, Malcolm Donnelly abandoned Glasgow as a fictional setting. His subsequent novels, *Queen of the Narcos* and *Jazz Vendetta*, published after four- and five-year intervals respectively, were set in Harlem, Peru and Nigeria, and saw a return to the fantastical storylines and buoyant mood of Donnelly's earlier work. He died in 1999, following complications of the large intestine.

Fredrick Mulligan, *Life in Flames*

Bald and toothless apparently from early manhood, Limerick-born Fredrick Mulligan was hardly the most handsome of Irish writers, but he did manage to invent (and exhaust) a new fictional genre, the so-called 'Paddy-slasher'. His influences were mostly non-literary – indeed, in his only traceable interview (which he gave to a short-lived magazine named *Tuning Fork*), he claimed never to read at all. 'Books are a quare thing,' he said. 'A French fad, surely. I only got into writing because any fucker can do it. All you need is a pencil.' Mulligan drew inspiration from the 'video-nasties' of the early eighties, and such directors as Dario Argento, Abel Ferrara, George A. Romero, and especially Ruggero Deodato (of *Cannibal Holocaust* notoriety).

Mulligan left Limerick at nineteen and spent the subsequent decade in London, working on the sites, drinking copiously, and having affairs with anyone who came into his purview that would look past his formidable ugliness. 'Women, men – never gave a bollox,' he later explained. For three years he shared a house in Kilburn with five or six other young Irishmen. Then he moved into a basement bedsit north of Kentish Town. It was in that cramped bedsit, by lamplight after hard days on the sites, or hungover at weekends, that Mulligan wrote his collection of short stories, *Hounds of Hell and the Rum-Beast of Kilmacud*, and his only published novel, *Slaughterchaun*. The stories and novel read like transcripts of early first-person-shooter video games such as *Doom* or *Wolfenstein 3D* (games which Mulligan never lived to see, but doubtless would have approved of). In *Slaughterchaun*, narrative thrust is eschewed in favour of unrelenting carnage, gunplay and mutilation. Jack, a muscular and sexually omnivorous Limerick farmer, blasts his way across a ravaged Ireland swarming with vicious and depraved faery-folk. Armed with a shotgun, a blowtorch and a haversack full of rudimentary explosives, Jack joins forces with Priest, a clergyman who has lost his faith after seeing his congregation decimated by the faery horde, their innards gorged upon and their corpses incinerated. 'God has left us?' roars the priest into a gully at one point. 'Very well, then I am the Black Christ of Annihilation!'

Dialogue is wooden and preposterous; characterisation non-existent. The climactic chapter, 'Mound of Corpses', has a body count in the hundreds, as wave upon wave of winged banshees, leprechauns and faeries descend from the blood-red skies upon our beleaguered heroes, who are now inexplicably perched on the summit of Carrantuohill. After hours of blasting, Priest turns the shotgun on himself, blowing out the tip of his spine after reiterating his contempt for God, church and man. Jack flees to a cave to re-gather his strength and draw up plans for a new resistance. The novel ends with a fevered prayer to the blackest gods of hate and vengeance.

Mulligan evidently intended a sequel. *Slaughterchaun*, alas, was to be the last book he ever completed. Aged thirty-one and jaded with London life, he returned to Limerick. He lived in a caravan in the countryside several miles outside the city, where he bathed every morning in a river, drank cheap flagons of cider, and made several attempts at a new novel, provisionally titled *Banshee Inferno*.

The words, however, would not come. Three nights before his thirty-third birthday, Mulligan wrote a few half-coherent lines on a page torn from a gay porn magazine, and pinned it to a nearby tree. Then he drank a bottle of whiskey, doused his caravan in petrol, lay on his bed wearing only a pair of boxer shorts, and incinerated himself.

Banned on first appearance, Mulligan's books have never been published in Ireland to this day.

Martin Knows Me – the Lonely Struggle of David Haynes

Failure can be a kind of career. Bitterness too. Unlike most young Irishmen who emigrated to London in the eighties, David Haynes went not in flight from a barren economy (he left behind steady work as a reporter at the *Derry Star*, where he had covered the arts, sports and agriculture), but as a literary pilgrim. Enamoured of contemporary English writing, Haynes's most ardent devotion was reserved for Martin Amis, whose career and personal life he followed avidly. Harbouring dreams of becoming a fiction writer himself, Haynes believed that London would provide a more amenable backdrop for such a project than his troubled native city.

Living alone in an apartment off the Charing Cross Road overlooking Soho, Haynes spent many evenings during his first years in London rereading all the Amis novels that had then been published. Determined to grasp the sorcery of the master's style, he would type out the novels in their entirety on the typewriter he used for his journalism. By day, when he wasn't writing articles or chasing down sources, he would walk the streets, alleys and inner city parks evoked in Amis's feverish fictional universe.

After three years in London, Haynes lost his job at the *Irish Post*, where he had written on various issues of interest to the London Irish community. Taking a job as a waiter at Berconi's, an Italian restaurant in Soho, he decided that the interruption to his journalistic work was an opportunity to focus on his literary ambitions, which until then had remained largely nominal.

The novel that resulted from this decision, *Martin Knows Me*, was rejected in its early drafts by nineteen publishers in the UK and eight in Ireland. A smattering of phrases amid the rejection letters, suggesting mild interest in Haynes's future output, sufficed to keep his determination alive: he kept on writing. Working each night at the restaurant until two or three, Haynes would return to his flat, fix a cafetière, and write for five or six hours. Then he would read a little, and sleep until it was time for the evening shift.

Though he made several attempts to move on from *Martin Knows Me*, Haynes's unpublished first novel continued to tug at him. He believed in the book, or at least in its potential – to abandon it would be traumatic. In the earlier drafts, Martin Amis had appeared as a distant, ambiguous figure, haunting the thoughts of the sensitive and ambitious narrator (also named Martin), as he came of age against an oppressive backdrop of sectarianism and narrow-mindedness: Amis was an emblem of the young man's yearning, disaffection and thirst for culture (or merely glamour). In later drafts, the novel's tone is considerably darker: the plot now involves a troubled writer who moves to England seemingly with the intention of *becoming* Martin Amis, or possibly murdering or sleeping with him. Though these later drafts contained, in the words of a young female intern at a literary agency to which Haynes submitted the typescript, 'some uncomfortable insights' and 'moments of real skill', they failed to attract much attention.

Seven years had passed. David Haynes was still in London, still waiting tables, still unpublished. He was now in his mid-thirties, no longer a young man, and with little to show for it. Over the course of a harsh winter, the truth, buried for so long beneath the furies of work and the late-night chatter of his typewriter, pushed itself to the surface: Haynes could not write.

At least, he could not write like Martin Amis. The revelation was the trigger for a prolonged psychic unravelling. More than once, Haynes found himself weeping helplessly while standing in the kitchen at Berconi's, embarrassing nearby chefs. In his apartment he would sit for hours by the window, gazing into the darkness till a dreary sunrise filled out the cobbled sleaze of Soho. During this period, Martin Amis was at the summit of his powers and acclaim, before the dethroning he was to undergo in the nineties. Haynes could no longer bear to read anything by or about Amis – too lacerating were the reminders of the glamorous life and mercurial talent, the precision and swiftness of intellect which would never be his.

Some months prior to his breakdown, Haynes had met a quiet, twenty-three-year-old German girl named Ann-Sophie, who had been working as an *au pair* in London. Haynes began writing to her more frequently, confiding his distress at the possibility of seeing himself as an utter failure. Through their correspondence the two became very close, and before long it was decided: Haynes would move to Heidelberg to be with Ann-Sophie.

Though the outline of a new future was becoming visible, Haynes needed to feel some sense of closure. Several days before moving to Germany, he resolved to go and see Martin Amis, who was due to give a talk at Kings Place in Islington. On the night of the event, Haynes arrived alone and sat near the back of the auditorium, which filled to capacity. There was a surge of anticipation as the lights dimmed – it was enough to muffle the sound of Haynes's first gasp, his first sob. Amis walked on stage, sat down in a leather chair, and began speaking.

Afterwards, Amis sat at a table in the foyer to sign books. Haynes joined the queue, determined if not to speak to Amis, then at least to stand before him and look him in the eye. Perhaps in that way he could convey some inkling of the ardour, the ecstasy, the sorrow he had known.

When there were only four bodies separating him from Amis, Haynes's nerve failed: he ducked out of the queue and hurried away, out of the foyer and into the street. He walked through London one last time, intensely aware of the city night, its monstrous poetry; he knew that once he left this place, he would never return.

David Haynes moved to Heidelberg, where he married Ann-Sophie. They went on to have two children, Romaine and George, and ran a café that proved popular with students. Apart from the odd poem, which he chose not to show to anyone, Haynes never wrote again.

The Turk Inside

She came to London when she was twenty-one. Now she's older, I doubt she lives in London any more but I can't be sure (she deleted her old email account, changed her phone).

She got work as an exotic dancer at a club near Russell Square. It was expected of all the girls there that they slept with the owner, the manager and probably another rank or two along the pecking order as well. The owner was an oily, brutal Turk. As you know, people come to London to make money, they stamp on other people and they laugh about it, never any remorse. It's horrible, unbearable.

She slept with the Turk, he gloated over it. That's the kind of man he was. There's no moral to this story, no kind of comeuppance at all. The Turk is happy still. He abides in splendour and he's slept with more women than you or I ever will, despite his ugliness. I think of this man as a harvester of souls. He is my shadow self, the projection of my own shrieking, sick and mutilated will to power. I'm a total fucking wreck. He is me, on some level. The Turk.

She slept with the Turk. Him first and then me. She was very beautiful (I think she still is). She had a room in a flat in Canary Wharf that seems, when I picture it, to have had no windows in the corridors, only a warm electric light. She was on the nineteenth floor. There were some nights in there, and mornings across the river with croissants and coffee, looking back over open waste ground at the clustered skyscrapers of the business district. I wasn't in love with her. Then I was, but it was too late because I had scared her, or she just felt scared, which in the end are one and the same thing. The tables had turned. Life is like that, and there's nothing funny or poetic about it. More like a mockery.

One night, when I was still with her, I went to watch her dance. I didn't tell her I was coming. I sat down the back, almost in disguise, hidden behind my drink, in the shadows. Maybe she saw me, what do I know. Really – and this is probably clearer to me now than it was then – really I was looking for the Turk. I hardly even concentrated on her dancing, though I admit it was beautiful (what I saw of it), her pale young body bathed in the blue light, called forth to radiance from the grime and neglect and all that her father could never protect her from. She had many admirers that night, but I never caught a glimpse of the Turk. Maybe he's backstage, I thought desperately, draining my drink and wiping my lips as she bowed, then stepped serenely from the podium, and out through the narrow doorway.

I got home that night at three a.m., drunk and furious. Bitter, bitter. I masturbated savagely to web-porn and slept with the come not yet dried on my knuckles.

The next day I saw her, I mean we met up, first for a cappuccino, then an autumn afternoon stroll through Hyde

Park, where foreign students walk dogs by the dozen (I hear they make decent money). Every man we passed seemed not only to seek out her eye, but to grin a faint, smug grin, like they were all in on some joke and I was the only one left in the dark. I kept it in, I said nothing, I was fucking chivalrous.

Another time we were back at her place in Canary Wharf – the nineteenth floor, London down there like a plane of stars, or neon smears, or just science fiction. And how many cameras are down there, and not one of them ever saved me from anything. We screwed and I tried to memorise the flaw-less orbs of her breasts, the way the light caught her body – it felt as if, for once in life, all the promise of pornography had been delivered, there was nothing left to be bitter about. But I kept thinking about the Turk, and then it's like my dick felt smaller, somehow not wide enough to fill her up, to give her the friction that she wanted. It was an illusion, I suppose, but at the time it seemed real enough. I stayed the night and then I had to put in a shift at the Mexican restaurant, wearing that fucking sombrero. It was an alright shift, though, cause Celak was there and we had sly laughs about pretty customers, and got decent tips. After work we went for a few drinks. Celak wanted to go clubbing in Tiger Tiger, but at eleven I said I had to be somewhere (it makes you feel important, it's never true, even when you think it is). I said see you man, and took a bus. This time I sat closer to the stage, more openly, and I drank more too, and I was kind of short with the waitress cause Jesus, I'm paying here, I'm the customer, what the fuck *is* this.

She came on after a Latina woman with a nice enough body but too old, too old. This time I watched her appreciatively and I even forgot about the Turk, more or less. She used one of those long, white, glittery things – what's it called, a boa? Is it called a boa? Or is that just a fucking snake.

The blue light, the music. Oh you are wondrous, I thought, and the men there all agreed, and she caught a few of their eyes, and I'd say that smile was a little less than professional, wouldn't you agree now, honey. When she headed backstage, I put my drink on the bar (empty) and tried to follow her in by another route. That didn't really work out, but it could have been worse and I left, as they say, unmolested. That night the porno I put on depicted weird metal devices and blood (fake probably), and a sinister font. I was ashamed in the morning but it had suited my mood.

For a couple of months we met up once or twice a week, we had sex, we saw a gig in Brixton. But always when I was with her the Turk invaded my thoughts – he *molested* me. Whenever we drank, things turned ugly. My mind twisted up, I hissed or snapped and said brutal or double-edged things, and basically upset her, but later I always apologised in a gush of sentiment and horniness (I could never walk away – an ass like that?). One morning we slept late and she woke up and said shit, I have to get going, hang around here if you want. So I did hang around, up on the nineteenth floor (thereabouts). I did what you'd expect: sniff her underwear, scrutinise the toilet bowl, pull myself off in her bed. I was going to somehow pretend I'd gone home, then hide under the bed and wait – I wanted to see if she'd bring him back. But in the end I thought the better of it, or really I couldn't be fucked. I let myself out, slid the key under the door like she'd said, and took two buses home. I got drunk that night and wandered late along Seven Sisters where it's busy, hoping for I don't know what, some kind of new horizon, a human reaction, some friendship I suppose.

When she broke up with me I sort of went off the radar for a while – I mean even to myself. I have trouble saying exactly what happened in those weeks, what I was up to. That wasn't only down to finishing with her: it had a lot to do with mephedrone, which was still legal then. You could just walk into a head shop and buy it. And I did, I walked right in there and bought it. It was so much better than coke – stronger buzz, more reliable, longer lasting, only a tenth the price. Coke is a status sign, you only get symbolically high, like Holy Communion.

Everything accelerated with the drug. I was all over London like a streak of red light in one of those stop-motion panoramas in music videos (the singer always moves at normal speed while everything rushes around her, she's supposed to be special; but everyone feels special, that's the primary con). I was living amid extreme, daily agony, blunted only by drugs and drink. The worst part was that I felt we hadn't had enough sex. That might sound crass or shallow, but I felt it as a real loss, it really *hurt*. You know you'll carry it with you till the end, that remorse – you failed to live to the full, life was for the brave and you did not make your moves.

She said I was too intense, that's why she broke up with me, she said I came on too strong – those kinds of clichés. In other words: same stuff they always say. They can't handle it, they say they want the high romance but really it's just security and families. So yes I was angry. But the thing is, I wasn't really that angry with *her* – or only in an indirect way. What really boiled my blood, what kept me awake at night, was not her, but … the Turk. Still. I'd wake up at 2:49, 4:06, 5:20, and I'd *know* – I can't explain how, I was just dead certain that at that very instant, over the other side of the city, he was lashing it into her, I mean searing out her insides, making her come again and again and again and again. And all the time he had that superior smirk, and he didn't take off his clothes (grey suit and jacket). And every thrust he gave her, every shuddering orgasm he brought her to – that was really *him fucking me*. That's all there is to it. Absolute injustice. I had no power whatsoever. I remember clawing my hair and my scalp, hissing and writhing around and making all these animal noises, grunts and shrieks, and moaning weird obscenities, racist invective, all kinds of random taboo stuff. It was like demonic possession. I wanted to kill him. I thought about it so much, I mean obsessively, just smashing his mouth in with a hammer and stomping his head to a mush, hacking into his face with a cleaver, the usual.

Celak was my only friend in those dark days. He didn't drink much, and looked down on my drug-taking with Muslim smugness, or wherever he comes from. But he was mad for women, so he came out with me every night after work. I'd be fucked off my head on meow meow, with my eyes like saucers, talking too quick, too eager for any human contact or approval, and Celak would be there at my side going sure, man, sure, but really his eyes were scanning relentlessly for women, flitting from one to the next, like RoboCop, sorting out their bodies and arses, catching their glances. A machine he was like. I always dreaded him actually picking up a girl, cause then I'd be out there on my own, stranded at four a.m. with nothing to go back to, nothing to stave off the shocking grief of the comedown but a dismal box room in a house full of strangers.

I came through that period, somehow. I mean the worst of it. The pain was still there, every day it burned. When things got a little clearer I was surprised to find I still had my job at the Mexican restaurant, despite all the sick days and lates and 'alienating or inappropriate behaviour', or however they put it in those fucking letters. But then I decided to go back, just once, and see her dance. I hadn't heard a word from her now in maybe two months. (I'd made a routine of calling her and letting it ring out, then calling her again, repeating that around twenty-five or thirty times per night.) On a Friday night I took a tube to Russell Square. I paid in and sat at a middle table, not too far from the stage.

All night I sat there. I must have seen a dozen dances – a redhead, the Latina woman, two blondes, a Chink with mad tits. When the same girls came out for a second rotation I knew she wasn't going to appear. I waited anyway, just in case. Her or the Turk, I had to see one of them. I knocked back a barrel's worth of whiskeys and Coke – they cost a fortune but I had to deal with the rage, though to be honest the drink only exacerbated it. I saw how the men were transfixed by the dancers – a flesh trance, a lust rapture. I imagined very vividly how the Turk had watched her just like that, except it was different cause he'd have trembled in anticipation, knowing he could have her the moment she stepped off stage. The images bombarded me, worse than ever. I let out a long moan and bit into my knuckle. I wanted to run outside, but where to? – the hell was inside me. I gasped at the waitress for more drink, I must've spent a week's wages, no exaggeration. I heard myself moan like I was dying. The fucking Turk, I gasped, loud enough for some guy to turn and look. And the awful truth of it was that what made her knees weak, what made him *better* than me, was his fucking money, his power, his prestige. The fucking Turk.

At some point I just wasn't in control any more and that's when I was shoving my way through the stage door, demanding that I be allowed to see her, getting slammed by a big black guy. She's *my* boyfriend, I roared – precision was lost in the rage – she's *my* boyfriend and you're saying I can't see her. I don't remember the actual getting thrown out but I assume they were civilized enough – I mean no broken bones or anything. Who knows what happened with the rest of the night, but it ended with me being shaken awake by a homeless man with grimy dreadlocks who looked genuinely worried. Dawn had broken and I was down on one of those smelly grey pebble beaches on the Thames, right in the heart of the city, on the South Bank, where they have raves in the summer. It was a dull morning and my pockets had been thoroughly looted. One shoe was missing, along with the sock. I still had on my leather jacket.

That night scared me. I had the realization – right there on that slope of grey sand by the Thames – that there was no getting away from the Turk, I mean the Turk inside, the *inner* Turk. Things had to change or I was fucked. I could be a waster no longer, the humiliation was too severe. It took some time, a few years I mean, but eventually things started coming together. Then, for a dark and frightening period, there was the cocaine instead of mephedrone, and all that led to, the regressions and setbacks – but that's another story, or I can't be bothered to tell it.

And so here I am, still working hard – too hard, I sometimes think, even my manager says I should take things a little more lightly – up in my office on the twenty-eighth floor, right bang in the City. It's still a struggle, I take one day at a time. I don't like to think about that other period of my life, but it comes back at night when I can't sleep, or early in the morning, before my first double espresso.

As for her ... I only saw her once after that – my breakdown or epiphany or whatever you want to call it. I was still fairly frail at that time, shaky. I'd lost the restaurant job, had no money, had fallen out of contact with Celak – I was basically litter on the breeze, too weak for life. I was sitting on a bench in Hyde Park. It was a summer's day, I forget why I was there, possibly no reason, just sitting and waiting. I looked up and saw her walking towards me along the pathway, it was too late to get up and scurry away. Beside her was a man – one of those bulging, all-in-black, fashion-beard guys with sunglasses, from Italy or the Middle East, wherever. I mean someone who was in love with himself, and you could tell right off that his phone cost twice your yearly salary. It was an awful moment. I shrank into the bench, hands in pockets, praying to God she wouldn't stop and talk, just walk on and pretend she didn't see me. But then she *did* walk on – and she'd seen me alright, I caught the moment of confusion and dismay on her face before she averted her eyes – and it was the most crushing, humiliating thing I'd ever experienced, like being informed I had a terminal sex disease or I was a leper. They walked away. I looked up when they were twenty yards on – she was under his wing, that rippling, designer-labelled hulk of muscle and self-worth. I stayed there on the bench, on my own. It occurred to me that there was no one, not a single person in this whole city, who I wanted to talk to at that moment, despite the suicidal loneliness. I stayed sitting there on the bench as the park slowly emptied out, and grey clouds drifted in across the sun, chasing away the warmth. Then the day was gone and all the people had left, just a few pigeons shuffling about. Finally the man with the green uniform and the rubbish prong came and told me to go home, or move away, or get lost, I don't really remember exactly.

Final Email from P. Cranley

*What follows has only the most oblique and tenuous of
claims to fictionality, being an email, transcribed from
memory, sent to me by an Irish friend I met while travelling
in India several years ago. Though the original is no longer in
my inbox, having no doubt fallen victim to one of my peri-
odic, over-vigorous purges, P. Cranley's strange last email,
which I received in late 2010 or early 2011 and read a great
many times, remains fresh in my mind. Its fractured and
torrential cadences still haunt me, as does the memory of
Cranley himself – a generous, likeable man who exuded the
unmistakable aura of being both doomed and psychotic. If I
have not achieved here a verbatim transcription of the email,
I have come close to it. Cranley never responded to any of my
subsequent attempts to contact him. In all probability he is
now dead.*

From: P. Cranley
To: Robert Doyle (No Subject)
4:32am

i did what i said i got out of st patricks hospital i came to america. my ma keeps emailing DONT DO IT WE LOVE U and da as well WHATEVER HAPPENED TO U WEELL FIX IT but i have to meet the angel. i know u laugh but only transcendent presence can save u me or anyone. u must embrace it. have u done so

let me tell u i

i came here 2 san francisco i checked into v cheap & v grimy hotel on colombus street which is bad-energy area where u will find titty bars. d guidebook say 'this area is OK by day but can be dangerous at night when it is often d site of drug deals and also cannibal hordes roam freely feasting on christians and yes d policemen have red SATAN eyes and truncheons of fire. with d truncheons they impale u anally in their HQ which is d COCK FORTRESS.' but i stay in at night i pray i write i have to meet the angel at 3 am tomorrow thursday out at d panhandle. this is dark strip of grass and benches where homeless wander nocturnally with shopping trolleys stocked 4 d coming holocaust. i pray i write i reread d lives of saints. st teresa of avila her story is my own. tears of fire 2 cleanse us of sin. but at night now she comes 2 me and whispers DESPAIR CHIL'', THE SKY IS A DESERTED QUARRY OR A FAMISHED MOUNTAIN THE LORD IS A CRIPPLE HE HATES US ALL. i cry i scream LIES but d other guests shout through d walls in spanish or gigolo & d manager pounds on door sayin QUIET OR U GET THE HELL OUT i know he is a denizen of d Foul Realm but i am protected in d ring of light holy light. embrace d lord in yr heart.

everything has changed

i need to explain all 2 u. starting. only with d force of god i
could walk out of that so-called hospital ie 'loony bin' (prison
of light. black cage of spirit ... bureaucrats of d abyss) i came
to san francisco like i said to meet d angel. of mercy of truth
... o holy fire. & yesterday i went down to castro where d
homosexuals congregate i roared BROTHERS I LOVE U AALL
BUT FEAR THE FLAME ... D LORD WILL SPEAK AND HIS
VOICE IS FLAME & U WILL TREMBLE & REPENT. YES. TO LUV
A MAN IS NOT A SIN BUT IT IS A TRANSGRESSION I TOO
HAVE MY SINS BUT I ACCEPT D LORD INTO MY HEART.
D RECKONING IS AT HAND & they were all laughing and i
wasnt d only 1 naked there was 1 homosexual male in cowboy
hat & nothing else he tried to dance with me while other
homosexuals clapped & cheered. i felt ridiculed i pulled on
'pants' AKA trousers and ran away ... angel will protect me i
felt strong and elated & ran to haight. nearby a music festival
ie. gathering of dark shamans/infiltration of d invader force.
but it was ok until i see this hippy ie 'human wreckage' with
a sign held up saying MELT ME. that i could not handle i ran
to d end of haight every1 deformed every1 doomed the armpit
of the earth i came to golden gate park at the end of haight/
hate & sat & cried. overcome i was d universal sorrow. could
not stop crying. like FATHER WE ARE SCREAMING COME
TAKE US AWAY OUR EARTH IS FALLING THROUGH SPACE
& SHAMANS MASSED IN LEGION FROM D FOUL REALM R
POISED TO OVERRUN BUT I HAVE NO FEAR OF D COMING
WAR IF U LUV ME DO U LUV ME d hippies gathered around &
took pity but i can see these are d broken children/orphans of
d american wilderness d broken west i see them all marching
into d ocean or a JAW in d sky. they have no teeth & crack-
head mothers tried to abort them & now they smoke chillum

& pray to universal spirit or ganesh or vishnu or shiva but i was frighten they had been duped n under d sway of d dark shamans from d far side of d universe where hate is d only law & cruelty d only science (vast technologies shown 2 me by d angel ... planet systems wholly of prison torture experiment/entire races engineered & raised captive only purpose as subjects of torture. they have elongated life & amplified nervous systems x1000000000 sole purpose is 2 feel agony) all of this is real

then d hippies were laughing to themselves while i was sitting there crying & 1 of them says to me HEY MAN WHAT U NEED IS SOME SHROOMS they all laughed & i knew they were conspire but then i look up & 1 hippy girl she was smiling at me benign smile i knew she was different she was beautiful & then i knew 'it is a sign!' she was d angel or a human bodiment of d angel 2 guide me through d utter chaos. calm i put out my hand n d hippy reached out & put d mushrooms in it i ate them. d other hippies were laughing & watching like v curious & then d shroom guy took out more i ate them & then d other hippies weren't laughing & 1 says SHIT MAN, THATS 2 MUCH HE IS GONNA TWEAK ... YR A FUCKIN ASSHOLE & i felt fear. i start 2 panic but i thought 'look 4 d angel' so i looked up into crowd of hippies 4 d radiant girl but she was gone. & now i felt pure alone like had been duped & she was not d angel she was a trickster 4 d dark shaman. d other faces crowded around sneering & deformed. i screamed WHAT DID U GIVE ME WHAT HAVE I EATEN U CUNT i leapt i claw his face he screaming & blood flow i scream U DARK SHAMANS D LORD WALKS WITH ME I HAVE NO FEAR & put my finger in his eye. in d commotion i run so fast away from d park i kept running till they gone behind me. already i could feel d alien presence in my system this was d mushroom i knew it was Malign Presence i was crying 2 d angel 'PLEASE BE WITH ME NOW THIS IS MY TRIAL' i ran 2 a place called buena vista park a big mountain in d city. ran up d side of d mountain & all around me were screaming devils & d sky was a holocaust. i saw now that nature was a virus from d FOUL REALM and d virus has spread to everything. this was a revelation. nature not benign: d trees grass sky insects birds & animals r all manifestations of d FIEND & d FIENDs body is nature itself. i was in horror. nowhere 2 escape 2. i knew despair because i reached d top of d mountain & no one around & thick fog came rolling in across d bay i saw it swarm over d land & cover everything i saw d earth swallowed up in fog i screamed now i knew i had been fool all along. d great war 4 d earth is not to come IT ALREADY HAPPENED WE R LIVING IN D FOUL REALM ... IT IS CALLED NATURE ... WE LIVE IN D BODY OF SATAN i fell on d ground & cried i thought 'i am abandoned for ever in d body of satan' a dog came to me he lick my face i try to annihilate him i punch his face he shrieked & run he is 1 manifestation of d FIEND & i howled and screamed & then d vision overwhelmed ... planet in space. planet/Gaia is Satan & conscious & we are his serfs god is defeated & crushed & great war will never come we r lost. r future is 2 be engineered ie. earth as infinite suffering realm ie. warfare/ torture/screaming 4ever 2 feed d power of Satan

but when i had been crying 4 hours & lost everything i hear a voice. it is d angel she says SON YES IT IS DARK NOW U HAVE SEEN D TRUTH. D GREAT LONELINESS ... THERE IS NO LOVE THERE IS NO HOPE ... CRUELTY HAS WON U MUST ACCEPT THIS. D FATE OF D EARTH IS DECIDED. EARTH IS NOW HELL BUT IT IS STILL POSSIBLE FOR U TO LEAVE D EARTH. U MUST DESTROY D BODY & THEN I WILL TAKE U FAR AWAY IN SPACE. A SMALL BLUE PLANET WHERE D

LORD JESUS LIVES IN EXILE. THIS IS ALL WE HAVE LEFT. I AM SORRY 4 EVERYTHING. IT IS NOT 2 LATE. U WILL COME TO ME TOMORROW NIGHT. WE WILL DESTROY D BODY & LEAVE D EARTH I WILL TAKE U FAR AWAY FROM HELL

& then a peace came on me. still on d mountain i was surrounded by devils. but they were silent now. i stood up & walked among them i came down from d mountain i was not crying any more. i said to myself 'give 2 satan what belongs 2 satan. d world can not be saved. my loved ones & many more will remain in hell. d earth is preparing now 2 become full actual hell this will happen in december 2012. d war 4 d earth has already been lost.' i was resigned to this

i tell u this because 4 my ma & da & Jennifer it is 2 late. they will be put into Pain Machine & howl 4 billions of years. but d angel told me it is possible 4 u 2 leave d earth in time. rob it is not enough 2 die. u must destroy d body *& then b transported*. 4 this u will need d angel. first u must accept jesus in yr heart. he is far away & he has failed us but he can help u 2 escape from d coming holocaust

i can not help u any more. i am trying u must listen. time is short. v short. open yr heart. world is Satan but there is new home in deep space & i going there. u will hear no more from me rob. i will pray for u though. i am going 2 meet d angel

Jean-Pierre Passolet, a Reminiscence

When Jean-Pierre Passolet appeared at the door of his flat on a bright February morning in 2010, his loneliness was palpable. Still a thin, fragile-looking man, but with hair whiter than in the photographs, Passolet was living in a dismal council block far from the centre of London – the same flat in which he would be found, two years later, decomposing in his armchair. Driving out there that February day to interview him, taking in the dreary concrete anonymity into which London deteriorates when you cut through the East End, I had thought about some lines from Passolet's lyric-essay, *The Territories*:

> These peripheral zones, out past the noise, out past the centre, are what death, what oblivion must look like. The high-rises, the rust and ruin, the choked canals and derelict playgrounds – all of it silent, all empty and barren, as though deserted. The people seem barely real. Only a ghost life, a sketched life, is

permitted here. Existence is a waiting room, an antechamber to nothingness. The people understand this, and so it is never spoken about. No one writes out here, and nor should they.

Passolet, I knew, had moved out there because it was all he could afford. His sales had never been great, even during the peak of his acclaim, in the early nineties when *Heaven* and *European Graveyards* were published within a year of each other. By the time of my visit he'd long since given up the Hampstead house he'd lived in for several years with Lorraine Holden, his second wife, now divorced. I had gone there on the tube one Saturday afternoon to look at the old house, and to take some pictures. The contrast with his new dwelling was painful. There were even rumours that Passolet was on benefits.

When I turned up to interview him, Passolet was a few months shy of his fifty-eighth birthday. The publishing world had all but left him behind. Attracting few readers now, he had put out his last two books with a very small independent publisher which would never bring him near even the modest fame that had once been his. I was not sure that he cared very much about this; to me, though, this fading of Passolet's name, this premature obsolescence, was baffling and lamentable. Having first read him, in a trance of fascination, when I was eighteen, I considered Passolet a kind of unsung Sebald or Coetzee, a writer whose work was of a depth, intelligence and sustained, undemonstrative anguish that made him one of the most vital voices in contemporary letters. I hoped that the interview and the article I planned to write might do something to rehabilitate his reputation, and get people talking about him again (I was enjoying, at the time, a relative peak in my own visibility and influence).

Opening the door to his flat on the third floor, Passolet regarded me briefly before offering his hand and saying, 'Please come in.' His voice was how I expected it to be – parched, weary, strained, though not unkind – or not, I mused, without 'an obscene echo of kindness' (the phrase came to me from *European Graveyards*). His accent was glaringly uncorroded, even in those three words. The interior of the flat had a twilight ambience that I sensed was as perpetual as the dust that hung in the air, coating my throat and making me cough as soon as we stepped inside. Passolet led me into a sitting room cluttered with books (most of the titles were in French), printed pages, journals and tax forms.

I heard stirrings from the kitchen. A woman appeared in the doorframe, nodding politely at me before stepping into the hallway and closing the door behind her. 'My partner,' said Passolet. She was blonde, attractive, though her eyes were puffy and tired as if she'd been crying – intuitively I glimpsed the bitter fights they must have had, the insults and cruelty that probably made up their days. Perhaps, I thought, the miasma of loneliness pervading the flat was the kind that is heightened, not diminished, by the fact of two people's proximity. Passolet offered me tea, which I declined. I cleared my throat, feeling a little nervous. He was sitting opposite me, across a low wooden table. 'Shall we begin?' I asked. He nodded his head, gaze turned downwards.

I didn't waste time on what I already knew: Passolet's excruciating biography, the madness that had pursued him like some black awful wraith, ready to fall on him whenever he weakened. I knew about the psychiatric institutions he had staggered in and out of, an array of them pockmarking first France, then Belgium, and finally Britain. I knew about the 'rituals with candles and deranged prayers' he had performed during the nadir of his ordeal. And I knew what loomed behind it all: the sexual abuse he had suffered in his childhood, virtually every day for years, at the hands of his widowed mother's boyfriend, in the town of Amiens where he grew up. That had gone on till he was thirteen. It was all there, in the books he had written. So too was the teenage alcoholism, and the 'desperate appeal' to Catholicism which ended when, at nineteen, he first read Schopenhauer. He would describe this last event in *European Graveyards*:

> I turned the pages in a kind of ecstasy or annihilation ... The houses, the roads and buildings of that drab provincial town, and all the humans and institutions, and everything else fell away, as did the illusion that had sustained them, and I saw that I was falling, like everything else, falling through a limitless void, in slow-motion, without adhesion, the roar of an immense cosmic violence in my ears. But rather than terror, for the first time I felt blessed, liberated, relieved of the weight that had been crushing me all my life.

After this powerful encounter, Passolet gave up drinking and moved to Paris, where he began studying theatre in the Conservatoire National. Initially imagining he would become an actor, he lost interest in the idea after a few years and dropped out, but not before having made many friends in the Parisian avant-garde of the mid-seventies. 'People liked me because I wasn't there,' he later wrote. 'At least, not as a threat or a rival, which is how most men are condemned to confront one another. I was agreeable because I never felt I had the right to judge or despise anyone.' Despite his popularity, Passolet was still afflicted with depression and anxiety throughout these years, and was institutionalised several times. Somehow he managed to keep this fact, and the worst upheavals of his nervous condition, from his friends.

A woman in her fifties named Silvia Bresson-Levaint, the childless wife of a respected theatre director, developed a particular fondness for Passolet. They became close friends, and the Bresson-Levaints would invite Passolet to spend periods at their summer house on the shore of Lake Annecy, at the foot of the French Alps. It is there that Madame Bresson-Levaint encouraged the young Jean-Pierre to write. He had, in fact, been writing for several years, without any real direction or thought of publishing. 'I wrote from the right-brain,' he later recalled. 'That is, from the dream-channel, the imagistic source into which one descends after falling asleep ... What I wrote was shit, really, but it was the beginning, the scratchings at a surface I would spend decades excavating.'

Silvia Bresson-Levaint was the kind of woman who might have run a literary salon in an earlier era; she had many friends who were writers and artists, having earned a Master's at the Sorbonne and considered a career in academia before getting married. Jean-Pierre would accompany Silvia on walks along the shores of the lake, during which they would passionately discuss Schopenhauer, whose evocations of the suffering that coursed through existence resonated so profoundly with the young man. Madame Bresson-Levaint perceived in her friend an intelligence, a depth of feeling and a dexterity with words which she knew was rare and worth cultivating. She urged him to set down his insights with greater discipline and purpose.

Passolet had never told Madame Bresson-Levaint, nor anyone else, about the abuse he had endured years earlier. The memories of rape and violence still tormented him, triggering panic attacks so severe he had once tried to kill himself by hacking into his wrists. After an April day spent walking in the Alpine foothills, Passolet came to pieces while sitting by the fireplace with Madame Bresson-Levaint. 'It was as if a dam had burst inside of me,' he wrote, 'blown apart by the shock of a happiness that had asked nothing of me, had concealed nothing from me, and which therefore I found unbearable.' He unburdened himself of his past, and Silvia listened, distraught, while cradling the young man to her breast. The next day, having discussed the matter with her husband, she offered to let Jean-Pierre stay on at the lake house for as long as need be, so that he might try to confront or transmute his suffering, perhaps by shaping a book from his experiences. (The Bresson-Levaints had little faith in psychoanalysis, or psychotherapy in general, despite Silvia's friendship with Jacques Lacan. Previously, the couple had seen a close friend, a certain Madame Ducroix, kill herself with pills and wine despite years of intensive and costly analysis.)

Passolet, who was twenty-two and otherwise without direction, accepted the offer. He lived by the lake for a year, alone but for the domestic employee, a thirty-year-old Algerian woman named Celine Begadour, and frequent visits by Madame Bresson-Levaint. The house was well stocked with literature, and Silvia would bring books from Paris which she felt would inspire Passolet. He read La Rochefoucauld, La Bruyère and the moralists; the essays of Montaigne (which moved him almost as much as Schopenhauer had); Proust; Pascal; Hegel; Sarraute and the *nouveaux romanciers*; the Sufi poets; the Gnostic scriptures of Nag Hammadi; almost the entirety of Freud, and much else besides. 'Most of the real reading I have done in my life, I did during that year,'he later claimed. He wrote each morning, and walked for hours by the lake and into the nearby forest, immersed in himself.

Although Madame Bresson-Levaint expected that he would use this period to write some kind of memoir or autobiographical novel, the book that was born of that solitary year turned out to be something very different. Set in an unnamed, mist-enshrouded country during a time of war, and populated by characters who appear and then drop out again without logic or pattern, only to reappear with different names and personalities, *Cities in Crystal* is one of the few novels I know deserving of that much-overused epithet, 'dreamlike'. It is also a singularly menacing read: although no violence or horror is depicted directly, it is impossible not to sense, on almost every page, the proximity of an intense, brooding malevolence. The elusive narrative is haunted by the presence of a beautiful, dark-haired woman with lines on her face suggesting a hard life and a fierce character. I had read in one of Passolet's interviews that, although this figure was undoubtedly an avatar of Celine, the woman who came each morning to cook and clean for him, and though he was, in fact, in love with Celine, he remained ignorant of either circumstance until long after the book had been published. 'Celine walked into my writing the same way she walked into my unconscious: quietly and unnoticed,' he said. In the novel's inexplicable final scene, the human characters all transform into birds – sparrows, hawks, peregrines and ravens – and fly together into the sky, ascending through the earth's atmosphere, dissolving finally in the beyond.

After a year, Passolet returned to Paris with the typescript of his first novel in his briefcase. It was not difficult for Silvia Bresson-Levaint to persuade a publisher friend to accept it. The book was a modest success and, with the royalties, Passolet rented a small studio apartment on the rue Garancière, near to the Jardin du Luxembourg, where he liked to take walks early in the morning. Though he had gained confidence since the publication, Passolet's success did not spell an end to his psychological turmoil. That winter, while working on an early draft of what would, almost a decade later, become his most famous book, *Heaven*, he suffered a crisis more severe than any that had gone before. After a volley of desperate, barely coherent letters and phone calls to his friends – though not, oddly, to Silvia Bresson-Levaint – Passolet disappeared. Unable to contact him, his friends (he had long been estranged from his mother and elder brother) had little choice but to believe he was dead, most likely by his own hand.

The truth was only marginally less unpleasant. Deranged by memories that assailed him now with greater virulence than ever, a dishevelled, unshaven Passolet wandered France for several months, sleeping rough, or in dosshouses patronised by alcoholics and low lifes. Several times he was taken in by the police and spent the night in a cell. He entered numerous psychiatric institutions, staying for as long as a month before checking himself out to wander once more without aim or destination. He relapsed into alcoholism as he drifted further beyond the limits of respectable society. At one point, he found himself staying amid a community of gypsies who were travelling slowly across the rural north of France. The gypsies tolerated him, for a few days at least, due to the wine he shared, bought with his now-dwindling royalties. One of the gypsies, a mustachioed and sullen man who held a certain status in the camp, and wore a white vest that he never seemed to change, became the object of Passolet's intense fixation. Every day, Passolet would watch him furtively, initially having no idea why the man exerted such fascination. Then the answer came to him: this man was the tormentor of Passolet's youth, the boyfriend of his mother who had sexually abused him so many years ago. It didn't matter that the gypsy looked nothing like the abusive boyfriend, nor that there would have been a huge difference in their respective ages: Passolet *knew* it was him, either in a cunning disguise, or altered due to some other whim or sorcery. This insane notion, which Passolet felt with the force of a holy revelation, left him terrified. He wept that night as he lay under a few rags in a clearing between two caravans, appalled by the injustice of having his tormentor reappear in his life, no doubt poised to inflict yet more misery on him. But then Passolet hardened, willing his tears to cease. Now was not the time for weakness and self-pity, but for manliness and bloody vengeance. Passolet would prove that his role in life was not that of a mere victim: he decided he would murder the gypsy. The next morning, he stole a heavy knife and concealed it in his trousers. He knew that the gypsy slept in the furthest caravan out from the road, along with his wife and three of his children. Passolet would enter the caravan while the gypsy slept, and plunge the knife into his neck. If the wife or children tried to stop him, he would slaughter them as well. Then, either the other gypsies would lynch him, or he would slash his own throat before they had the chance. Passolet was surprised by how calm he felt, now that the intention was fixed. That night, however, having drifted off while awaiting the optimal moment to carry out the murderous act, he awoke in aghast lucidity: he knew his plan was madness; the gypsy had nothing to do with him; he had never even set eyes on him before arriving at the camp.

Passolet fled that same night, terrified by what he had intended to do, the madness that had possessed him. He hurried by moonlight along rural back roads, imagining unspeakable forms pursuing him through the darkness. Eventually he reached a stream, which his intuition told him was a safe place – evil could not touch him here. He carved a cross in the earth with his stolen knife, then lay down and slept. When he awoke, the sun was shining in a clear morning sky. A faint breeze stirred the rows of corn growing alongside the grassy bank. Birds chirped, and the stream gurgled gently by his head. Passolet felt the warmth of the sun on his face; he knew that this warmth was the hand of the Lord, and that it offered solace, and deliverance from the devils within; he knew too that he had to prove his ardour to deserve this beneficence. Still lying on his back, Passolet took the long, heavy knife from out of his trouser pocket. With his left hand he unfreed his penis and stretched it out above him. He did not manage to sever the penis completely before he passed out; the damage, however, was enough to ensure he would be wholly impotent for the rest of his life. Passolet was found by a farmer's young son who was out cycling by the river, a bloody patch spreading from his groin. Had he been left there much longer, he would have bled to death.

Passolet did not write about this shocking episode for many years. I had agonised, while preparing to interview him, about whether I would bring it up, finally deciding that to do so would serve no purpose other than to feed the salacious curiosity I detested in both the press and myself. After being hospitalised, Passolet was committed to yet another institution, this one in an affluent Paris suburb, his lengthy stay there paid for by the Bresson-Levaints. Thus began the years of Passolet's long convalescence. Initially, he spent most of his days sitting out in the well-tended grounds of the institution, staring into space, or drawing childish pictures of obese cats with blank, circular faces. Silvia Bresson-Levaint often visited him, on occasion bringing Celine Begadour, who had recognized herself in the pages of Passolet's book. One spring day in 1986, three years into Passolet's stay, Celine brought along her young daughter, Beatrice. Passolet said little during the visit, but Celine would later recall, in conversation with a Belgian journalist, that tears had flowed down his face as the dark-haired little girl stood by his side, watching him curiously. Passolet later claimed that it was the sight of Beatrice, the trust and gentleness in her manner, which marked the beginning of his recovery. 'I could have killed her with my bare hands,' he said. 'But she had no fear of me, only this miraculous trust. That was very moving.' When Passolet finally left the institution a year and a half later, he sought out Celine to thank her for her visits. Discovering that Celine had been widowed some years previously, Passolet proposed to her. At first, she refused – Passolet was, after all, a man who had been institutionalised for years after committing a violent and inexplicable act. Moreover, he was impotent. Yet they remained friends, and Passolet persisted in his declarations of love. Seeing that he moved confidently again in his old social and literary circles (*Cities in Crystal* had grown in reputation during Passolet's convalescent years), and was in a position to provide for her daughter and herself, Celine eventually relented. They were married, and lived together in an apartment in the ninth arrondissement.

Now in his mid-thirties, Passolet enjoyed the first taste life had granted him of a normal, uncomplicated happiness. Re-accessing the creative fount that had been blocked throughout the years of his confinement, Passolet completed *Heaven*, the book he had started so long before, and immediately began what for my younger self was his essential work, *European Graveyards*. Published a year after *Heaven*, a realistic novel depicting the rapture and disintegration of a young Viennese pianist, the later work did not enjoy the same commercial success, but that came as a surprise to nobody. *European Graveyards* is a strange, difficult, cold book, which casts its affectless gaze across the darkest regions of the twentieth century, weaving historical vignettes with chillingly neutral depictions of Passolet's own madness and institutionalisation. (The penis-slicing episode is alluded to but not depicted; it would not be until his most straightforwardly autobiographical book, *Eggshells*, in 1999, that Passolet would write directly about it.) In one chapter, enclosed between essays on 'rock'n'roll terrorists' and the 'eternal howling' of the Dresden dead, the author Jean-Pierre Passolet has already died. In a suburban psychiatric institution – evoked as a Kafkan or Kunderan waiting room to a sinister beyond – Passolet's corpse is placed sitting in a chair, and various figures from his life – Celine, Beatrice, the Bresson-Levaints, the white-vested gypsy, his mother – enter the room to deliver monologues that touch on, but are not restricted to, their relationship with the deceased. A slender, faceless man in a tuxedo appears and announces that he has 'no quotidian penis'. He undoes his flies to prove it, whilst insisting that the fingers of his left hand are 'confident, slithering' penises. Another visitor is an extremely old woman whose body is in an advanced stage of decomposition; she does not say anything, just stands before Passolet's artificially shiny corpse for a very long time, as if waiting for him to speak. Finally the rotting woman mounts Passolet's corpse and begins straddling him, fucking him slowly at first, but soon reaching a violent climax – at which point her head falls off, rolls across the floor, and bursts into flames.

The book is too long – over six hundred pages – but there are moments of eerie, enigmatic beauty which, at least for my eighteen-year-old self, made it seem a devastating work of art. The final section was my favourite: in it, Passolet imagines the cities of Europe emptied of people; not in ruins, not razed or ransacked, but majestic in their desolation, as birds squawk and soar across hazed skies. 'The world has not ended,' he tells us, 'but people have faded away, and have done so will-ingly, with a lightness of spirit, a lucid joyfulness, as if walking collectively into a great chasm, a gaping maw.' This section, like so much in Passolet, is offered without explanation. It is not difficult to see why so many readers dismiss Passolet as a particularly glaring exemplar of French pretentiousness, of literary froth, but I have never shared this view.

Passolet was delighted by the reception that both books found among the French literary establishment. However, lasting happiness was never to be his fate. Within six months of the publication of *European Graveyards*, he and Celine were divorced. Celine successfully appealed for a restraining order to be placed on Passolet, barring him from seeing Beatrice or her. In court, she cited the growing signs that Passolet was relapsing into hallucination and irrational behaviour. ('Love', Passolet had written at another time, 'is itself a hallucination.') Within three months of the divorce, Celine had remarried, to a chef from a restaurant near the apartment she had shared with Passolet. Like so many men before him, Passolet took to the bottle in the aftermath of his wife's desertion, and appeared destined to sink once more into the chaotic life that Celine had done so much to lift him out of. In one notorious incident, he was beaten up outside a respectable Montmartre restaurant, having hurled anti-Semitic insults at a man who was dining with his eighty-nine-year-old mother (neither the man nor his mother were Jewish). Passolet had his jaw and nose broken and appeared in the French press under such headlines as 'Traitor to Literature' (*Le Monde*) and 'Go Back to the Madhouse, Jean-Pierre!' (*Le Parisien*). When, not long after this incident, Silvia Bresson-Levaint died following a struggle with breast cancer, Passolet felt he could not stay in Paris. He stopped drinking and moved to Bruges, where he taught an evening course in creative writing at the university. At a literary conference in London he met Lorraine Holden, remarried, and moved to the UK.

So began Jean-Pierre Passolet's steady decline into the obscurity and financial privation in which I would find him, many years later, when I turned up at his council flat in East London. Rather than probe him about the details of his life story, I wanted to talk with him about the work itself.

I had begun the interview by asking him a question concerning the enigmatic final section of *European Graveyards*. It was the kind of question I hoped would convince Passolet that he was speaking now with a real admirer, a young reader who possessed an intimate and impassioned affinity with his writing.

When I asked my question, though, Passolet only smiled abstractedly, lifting his head to gaze out the window, across the skyline. 'That book, yes ...' he said eventually.

As I waited for him to go on, noises reached us from the hallway; I heard the blonde woman leaving the flat. The silence resumed, persisting long enough for me to grow embarrassed. It was as if Passolet had forgotten I was there. Then he turned to me and said, 'You say you're from Ireland?'

I confirmed this.

'I met Beckett once. Did you know that?'

'No, I didn't,' I said, surprised.

Passolet nodded. 'I was twenty-one. I visited Mr Beckett in the company of a playwright friend who was acquainted with him. We sat in a bare, white room at a wooden table. Beckett made us sandwiches. I remember how he sliced the cucumbers; so very precisely, so thinly. I have never seen cucumbers sliced as thinly as that. They were the thinnest cucumber slices I have ever seen. Yes, such very thin slices ... A gracious man, Monsieur Beckett.'

I couldn't think how to respond. Perhaps sensing my perplexity, Passolet said, 'Did you say in your email that you were once a student of philosophy?'

'I was, yes.'

'Where did you study?'

'Dublin. Trinity College. The same place as Beckett, actually.'

He nodded. 'I mostly read philosophy these days. Very little narrative, very few stories. Through philosophy we can make friends with death. Through good philosophy, anyway. And that becomes very important. Do you know what Schopenhauer said? He said that the Upanishads had been the solace of his life, and they would be the solace of his death. That is beautiful. The Upanishads. He was the first one to open up the Western mind to all those things. Have you read the Upanishads?'

'Not really,' I said. 'Little bits.'

'You must. You must read the Upanishads. And reread Schopenhauer. He will help you to prepare for death. How old are you, tell me?'

'Twenty-nine.'

'Ah. Then you do not think much about death. A man only begins to think of death at thirty. That is when death first makes its presence known – not as the end of life, but as the irrevocability – is that the word? – yes, the irrevocability of the past, the realization that one's youth cannot be relived. But ah, forgive me. These words. I am happy you have come to see me. Few do any more.'

He said this, I thought, without bitterness, simply as an observation. I sensed it was better to remain quiet, not to force anything. I noticed that Passolet's lips were moving; he was frowning now, muttering inaudibly to himself.

I wondered whether I should say something. Then Passolet gasped faintly and closed his eyes. A moment later he said, 'The woman who you saw. Jacqueline. She has lived here with me for two years, nearly three. She is to me, I suppose, what the Upanishads were to Schopenhauer. But not always do I see it that way. I met her during a very unhappy time in her life. She is a magnificent woman. But Jacqueline ... Jacqueline always has been promiscuous, very promiscuous, ever since she was a teenager. In part this is due to the turmoil of her inner life, the pain she is in. But only in part. She is a nurse, she works in a hospital here which is like something one would find in Dante. She is thirty-nine now, and has slept with many, many men. She loves to sleep with men, to make love to them. She is the kind of woman, you see, who can reach orgasm very easily, and many times.'

He was watching me as he said all this – I couldn't conceal my embarrassment. He said, 'I am telling you this because I want to. I cannot talk about my books, not today. Perhaps, though, you will find some interest in what I say.'

I assured him, stammeringly, that I would listen to anything he wanted to tell me.

He nodded and went on. 'I will tell you something. Jacqueline did not sleep here last night. She spent the night with a man. This was not someone she had known before. It was a man she met at one of the nightclubs. I have never been to these places and I imagine them as something like the underworld. She came in at six o'clock this morning. The smell of him was still on her. So was the smell of her own sweat, her juices. You know, don't you, that I have been impotent since the age of twenty-four? Since what I did to myself. You have read it in my books. I ask Jacqueline about the men she sleeps with. This one was a large man, bald and with a beard, and tattoos on his biceps. He works as a mechanic, she said. When she came home this morning I made her recount everything they did together. All the close details. They took drugs together: cocaine. It sensitises her body. She rubbed it into his erection, to make it numb, so he will last longer. He

157

made her come six times in the night. Six times. When she told me all this I got up from the bed and wrote it down. I wrote about this man while Jacqueline slept with his seed still in her cunt. He is one of dozens. Last week there was a truck driver. A truck-driver! There have been many. Almost three years we have lived together. Sometimes she brings them back here, when I am away. She does not clean the sheets before I return. She is a beautiful woman, and she is a woman who enjoys sex. Men see that in her. It draws them to her. She prefers young men, in their twenties, thirties. Younger sometimes. They give her such great pleasure. And I consent to all this. Yes. I encourage it. But do not think that this does not cause me pain. I cannot describe to you how painful this is, when the woman I love so much, who is practically my wife, crawls into bed to get fucked by these men. These brutal, laughing men who light her body up like a firefly, like the fireworks I saw one night when I was crazy in Reims. When she tells me what she does with these men, I weep. I writhe in unsupportable pain. I feel so very worthless and small, like a battered foetus, unwanted, a foetus flushed down the toilet. Or a severed prick that is flung from a window on to a heap of rubbish, devoured by rats and spiders. And then I am cruel to her. I say things to her that would sicken you, things that would make you sick. You would be disgusted with me. But we love each other. This is our way of existing together. I write about these men who fuck her, who sodomise her; these men who get close enough to smell her shit, to see it on their pricks. I try to feel how this must be for *them*. Every one of them. Look.'

He gestured towards a stack of printed pages, a foot high, on the floor by the writing desk. 'That is only some of them. I will never publish any of it. Do you understand why I do this? Schopenhauer read the Upanishads and they taught him that death and agony are finally inconsequential, that we are fused with Being and therefore eternal. This lonely, unhappy man, he saw that the individual is only a figment, a ripple, but our essence is profound and cannot be compromised or lost. That was the salvation of this unhappy man, this rare, tragic German. And I write about these men, these young and virile men she sleeps with. Why should it matter if they fuck the woman I love while I lie here weeping? Why should it matter that I am broken, a eunuch, and they can light up this fire in her? I am these men. We are indestructible in our essence. In the depth of things there is no difference, no separation. There is not even pain, or pain is not worth anything, not worth lamenting, just a dream from which one must awaken. I am each of these men and they are I, as I am Jacqueline. Her bliss, her *jouissance* is mine. Or it is no one's. So you see, this is my practice, my spiritual practice. I am purging myself of an agony which is worthless, which persists only because I cling to a delusion that I am separate from this tattooed brute with his pierced phallus. I feel the pain of what she does to me, the burning humiliation. But one day I will not feel this pain, because I will see it for what it is – a delusion. Or perhaps the pain will kill me first; but at least I will die a good death, a spiritual death, a death worthy of the philosophers.'

When he finished saying all this, Passolet looked intently into my eyes – I felt a pleading, a desperation, as if he needed me not only to understand all this, but to affirm him in it: otherwise the whole edifice would crumble. If no one else could see virtue in his self-humiliation, he would be forced to confront an image of himself so stark, so pathetic, that the very sight of it would finish him off. But I didn't believe him; he couldn't convince even himself that he wasn't separate, wasn't alone, that his misery had some deeper significance.

Still he was peering into my eyes, pleading wordlessly.

I had to look away.

I didn't ask any more questions. Briskly I thanked Passolet and got up to leave. 'Yes, very good. I have talked too long,' he murmured, looking down, the confidence drained from his tone. The spell was broken; it was clear he regretted saying all he had said. Strangely, I now found myself wanting to linger there, to intensify his discomfort. I looked him in the eyes and imagined myself fucking Jacqueline, raping her over the sink while Passolet writhed in his chair, impotent and hateful. I wanted to dash his skull against the wall.

In the hallway, I stood by the door and shook Passolet's hand. I heard my own voice sounding coldly formal as I said goodbye. I left him on the doorstep, eyes turned to the ground, muttering again to himself.

Driving back to London, I already knew that I would not write the article about Passolet. I regretted having gone out there at all, though the cruelty that had welled up in me now subsided, leaving a residue of shame. Better to let the world's indifference bury him out there, I thought then; better to let him fade away, unmourned and unnoticed.

For a long time afterwards, I loathed Passolet. I told myself that his books meant nothing to me any more, felt no urge to put anything of him down on paper. I moved on from Passolet in the kind of brutal vanquishing we must inflict on our idols if we are to become what we are. It is only now, with Passolet dead, that my feelings towards him have changed, have relented. His body was found four months ago in his East London flat, badly decomposed, by a Romanian family living on the same floor. He had sat there for weeks, his starving cat chewing the flesh from his face and hands. I have no idea what became of his Jacqueline.

I don't know if I will ever read Passolet again, if I could re-experience the fervour his words ignited in me when I was young. Perhaps the most I can do to honour Passolet is strive to fulfil what he himself called the sole duty of the artist and the writer: to bear witness to the horror, and to the magnificence.

Acknowledgments

Thanks are due to the following people: Alexa von Hirschberg and her colleagues at Bloomsbury; Antony Farrell and his staff at Lilliput Press, especially Daniel Caffrey; Sarah-Jane Forder; Brendan Barrington; Dave Lordan; Alice Zeniter; Simon Kelly; and all those who generously took the time to read and comment on these stories at the various stages of their development.

The author gratefully acknowledges the support of the Arts Council of Ireland. Stories from this collection have previously been published in the *Dublin Review*, *gorse*, the *Stinging Fly*, the *Penny Dreadful*, *Penduline*, *Décapage* and Dalkey Archive's *Best European Fiction 2016*.

'Outposts' contains phrases snatched, often in truncated and/or altered form, from a variety of sources, including dreams, memories, Colm Tóibín, radio, Tõnu Õnnepalu, Georges Bataille, James Salter, television, Blaise Pascal, Desmond Hogan, conversations with patients at Saint Senan's, German Sadulaev, Roberto Bolaño, Virginia Woolf, Edmond and Jules de Goncourt, conversations overheard (or misheard) on the train between Rosslare Europort and Wexford town, E.M. Cioran, news websites, Yi Kwang-Su, James Joyce, Peter Coyote, Fyodor Dostoevsky, graffiti in a ghost estate on the Wexford coast, Georges Simenon, Albert Camus, Samuel Beckett, chants heard at a football match in Palermo when I hadn't slept in days, William Burroughs, Killian Turner, Andrei Tarkovsky, an abandoned novel set in Bangkok, my old notebooks, and Aka Morchiladze.